The Maze
in the Heart
of the Castle

The Maze
in the Heart
of the Castle

by Dorothy Gilman

Doubleday & Company, Inc.
Garden City, New York

Library of Congress Cataloging in Publication Data

Gilman, Dorothy, 1923–
  The maze in the heart of the castle.

  Summary: Consumed by grief after the deaths
of his parents, sixteen-year-old Colin accepts
the challenge of the maze of Rheembeck Castle
and begins to unravel the mystery of the maze
within himself.
  [1. Fantasy] I. Title.
PZ7.G432Maz 1983   [Fic]
ISBN: 0-385-17817-4
Library of Congress Catalog Card Number 82–45198

to Dr. Robert Savadove, with my thanks

The Maze
in the Heart
of the Castle

1

Colin was sixteen, a golden boy, when his mother and father died, both on the same day. Some said it was by a magic spell; others, by the strange plague that had descended on the country after the war with the Frolts and the curse that had been placed on the people.

Until that day Colin had never known grief. He had lived in ease and comfort, and expected nothing to change. He had been loved, too, wrapped in the great, warm, bearlike hugs of his father when he came home each evening from the fields, and by his gentle mother with her fragile beauty, who made each day as sunny and bright as the cloaks and tapestries she wove on her loom.

He was their only child, and now, suddenly, he was alone. Terrifyingly alone. And quickly enough he learned, too, that grief cast a spell of its own. It hurt. It hurt with a pain more searing than any arrow plunged into the flesh. In April that year every sign of spring brought fresh hurt because his heart was full of memories: of picnics beside Roaring Brook, of his mother telling him tales of the Old People or explaining to him about the herbs that grew in her garden (except there were none to heal his grief). He could not believe that his father would never again saddle his horse and ride beside him into the hills to show him rabbit runs and the nests of small birds on the cliffs. Sometimes a fragrance, a word, would catch him unexpectedly, and his heart would stand still until breath came back to him in a sob.

And then slowly—but more strong, even, than his grief—anger grew in him, and he would walk up Bald Hill to shake his fist at the sky and shout, "Why? Why this? How could you do this! We were so *happy*."

One day in his anger he saddled his horse, Black Prince, and rode down into the valley to the monastery where the wise men lived, or so his father had told him, one of them being Brother John, friend to his father since boyhood. Colin had to wait a long time for the priest because he was at prayers, but this made him sound a very holy man, so he waited patiently until Brother John hurried down the long corridor toward him, his brown robes flapping all around him. He had a rough, kind face, weathered and tanned from hard work in the gardens. He took Colin into his arms and embraced him.

"My poor boy," he said, "I'm glad you've come. I've said many a prayer for you. What a terrible loss!"

"Yes, and I want to know why," Colin said stormily. "I want to know why it happened. I've come to you to find out."

"Patience, patience," chided Brother John, and he led him to a bench to sit down. "All things come to an end, Colin, for you as well as for your mother and father, who have gone on to the Sky World. Nothing stands still—it was winter when they died, and look—now it is April and the wild flowers have begun to bloom."

"It was so sudden," cried Colin. "They weren't old, and they were good. Is there no justice, no kindness?"

Brother John sighed over his words. "It's not for us to know, Colin. We have to accept—accept what happens and go on."

Colin shook his head. "That's not enough for me. It's like burying something that needs to be looked at. I refuse to accept, I want to know why."

Brother John looked at him sadly. "In that direction lies madness, my son. It's not ours to know. If you can learn to accept, in time this madness will leave you."

"You cannot tell me why, then?"

Brother John shook his head. "But I can pray for you."

"Then is there no one—no one at all," cried Colin, "who can answer me? No one who understands or knows?"

"There is Hoveh," said Brother John simply.

"But He cannot speak!"

"He speaks in many ways," Brother John pointed out gently.

"Yes, He spoke when He took my parents away from me," Colin told him hotly, "so He is scarcely the one I can turn to now."

Brother John gazed at him for a long time and then said quietly, "There *is* someone who might help you—if he wished to. If you—" He stopped, and Colin saw that his eyes had a remembering look, as if his thoughts traveled far back in time.

"Who?" asked Colin eagerly. "Where can I find him?"

Brother John brought his gaze back to him, his eyes troubled. "You know of the old haunted castle on Rheembeck Mountain, certainly."

Colin shivered. Everyone knew of the castle. It was the stuff of which every child's ghost story was made. The mountain itself was forbidding, full of dark forests and a cliff that pierced the sky like a blunt knife. Somewhere near that crag stood the castle, they said, all in ruins now and haunted.

"There is an old man there, no one knows now when he came," said Brother John. "He's been called a ghost, a tramp, even a holy man, but he has been there for a long time, for as long as I can remember."

"Why do you say he might help?" demanded Colin. "Has anyone ever spoken with him?"

"I have," said Brother John, and Colin stared at him in surprise. "Once, long ago. Very long ago, when I was not much older than you are today."

Colin said in astonishment, "You met him, then. You were not frightened?"

Brother John shook his head.

"But what did he say to you?"

"He spoke of many things, and he offered me something—if I cared to take it," Brother John said softly. "I didn't—I felt I couldn't—and ever since I have wondered—it comes to me in the night sometimes—if I made the wrong choice." He shook his head. "But I had parents who needed me, it was impossible."

"But what did he offer you?" asked Colin.

Brother John reached over and affectionately ruffled Colin's golden hair. "Questions, questions! But you might try to find him, for I hear he is still there. The men who hunt wild boar on Rheembeck this spring have caught a glimpse of him now and then. Yes, he's still there. He was an old man when I met him, but there was something about him—I think he'd been old for a long time, perhaps he was born old, for I have come to believe that he is neither tramp nor ghost but a magician."

Colin said in astonishment, "I've never heard a priest speak well of magic."

Brother John laughed. "Blasphemy, do you think? But I've come to wonder if our god Hoveh and magic are really so far apart, Colin. Miracles still happen by the grace of Hoveh, do they not? And miracles are magic, are they not? Perhaps magicians reach out and touch that great Creative Flow that is Hoveh, and perhaps—who knows?— Hoveh loves their play and even shows Himself at times through them."

"If he is a magician," Colin said, nodding, "then perhaps he will take the pain away."

Brother John shook his head. "He would be a fool to do that, my son."

"What?" cried Colin, stung by such callousness. "How can you say such a cruel thing!"

Brother John smiled. "One day you will understand what I mean, Colin. For one thing, it's your pain that brought you here, is it not? And had you ever come to a monastery before?"

Colin shook his head.

Brother John chuckled. "It may even take you to the castle on Rheembeck Mountain, and there you have never gone, either. But I must leave you now, my boy." He stood, and politely Colin stood, too. As the priest looked at Colin, the man's gaze was strange and dark and unfathomable. "I wonder," he mused. "I wonder . . ." And then, very gently, he embraced Colin. "Whatever you choose, Hoveh go with you," he said, and abruptly turned and walked away down the long corridor, his brown robes flapping again at the haste of his stride.

He turned a corner and was gone, and Colin wondered why Brother John's voice had trembled when he said, "Whatever you choose, Hoveh go with you." In the garden, a bird began to sing and a small breeze stirred the grass. Colin straightened his shoulders and turned away, but he wondered why the feeling came over him that he would never see Brother John again.

Slowly Colin rode home, thinking about what his father's friend had told him. He rode through the village and up into the hills, cutting across meadows golden with dandelions and wild mustard, and when he reached Bald Hill he reined in his horse and for a long moment stared out across the Valley at Rheembeck Mountain. Even at noontime it rose dark against the sky, as sullen and brooding as his own heart. They were there-

fore well matched, thought Colin; he would go
there soon, and knowing this he put Black Prince
to a gallop.

Home was a sprawling stone house, too large
now and too empty, but this time as he approached it Colin felt no dread at entering. He
tethered Black Prince and went inside, up the
long curved staircase and into his father's
workroom. From the chest hidden inside the wall
he brought out fifteen gold pieces, dropping ten
of them into a leather purse and stowing these in
his pocket. Then he went to his own room and
brought out a clean shirt, the hand-loomed
sweater his mother had woven for him, and his
spare boots. He added his trusty, hand-carved
slingshot, some chalk for drawing, a comb, and a
penknife. These he wrapped and tied into a rain
cape.

Downstairs he found Huldah making soup in
the kitchen, and to her he gave the remaining five
gold pieces. "They're to keep you and Lahvo while
I'm gone," he told her, "because I have it in mind
to ride up into the hills for a few days."

She stared in awe at the gold pieces, and he
saw that she was suddenly filled with questions
and with doubt. To distract her he said in his most
imperious voice, "Now I will need lunch and a
dinner to take with me, Huldah, for I'm leaving in
just a few minutes. You can find food for me?"

"Food? What a question!" she told him indignantly, and immediately bustled about, the gold pieces forgotten as she pressed thick slices of meat between chunks of bread and added cheese, raisins, nuts, and a slice of rich cake. Last of all she brought out his father's two leather flasks, and poured tea into one and lemonade into the other. "Mind you take warm clothes with you," she told him sternly. "Spring may be here, but it's not reached the hills yet."

"Yes," he said, and showed her his neatly tied bundle. With a reassuring smile he blew her a kiss and went out to tie the two small sacks of food and clothes to Black Prince's saddle. Mounting his horse, he rode away.

Only once did Colin stop to look back, and it surprised him how small his home looked from the edge of the woods.

With an hour's hard riding Colin reached the foothills of Rheembeck Mountain, where he found and followed the ancient trails made by the hunters every spring. By the look of the sun he was another hour or more from home when he rode out of the deep, moss-floored forest to meet the crumbling walls of the castle resting against the crag. He tethered Black Prince at the edge of the woods and picked his way over the rocks to a wide, shallow staircase that led to a stone terrace. Once on the terrace he found that he could see for hundreds of miles around him, not only across the valley but beyond, to the shapes of unknown towns and even to the faraway mountains in the east.

As for the castle standing like a wall behind him—he turned, suddenly uneasy, and discovered that he was not alone. Where the man had come from Colin had no idea; he had not been there a moment before when Colin had walked up the stairs. He had simply materialized; he was there, an old man, as Brother John had promised, but with startling deep-set eyes as blue as sapphires glittering in the sun, eyes so penetrating they seemed to look at Colin as though he were transparent. The man's hair and brows were white and ragged, and so was the robe he wore, all patched with squares of color: purple, pink, orange, red, blue, green. Colin had never seen anyone like him before, but he was not frightened. He said, "My name is Colin."

"Yes," said the old man, "I've been expecting you."

Startled, Colin said, "How can that be?"

The man smiled. "I felt your thoughts when you stopped your horse on Bald Hill this morning and decided to come and find me."

"Then you really are a magician!" said Colin, pleased. "By what name are you called?"

"The Grand Odlum."

Colin said doubtfully, "That's not a name."

"It is in my country."

"And what country is that?"

The Grand Odlum glanced around. "There's absolutely no sense in our standing here when we can sit down on those stairs in the sun. Except I have to ask you not to sit close to me because your thoughts are terrible—all dark, violent, and stormy—which is very upsetting for me. From what country?" he repeated. "I'm the keeper of the maze that lies in the heart of this castle. Not too close," he reminded Colin sternly as he started to sit down.

"You really can feel my thoughts?" asked Colin.

"Feel them!" replied the old man. "I can see them as well. *Horrible* forms and colors. Terrible."

Colin very carefully sat at the opposite end of the staircase and called over to him, "But what's this maze you speak of? Where does it go?"

"It goes to a country not easy to reach and very far away."

"But what kind of country?" insisted Colin. "Do you come from there? Can others visit it?"

"Anyone at all can go," said the Grand

Odlum with a shrug, "but very few care to, and those who start out, being lazy, seldom reach the end."

"Is this what you offered Brother John?" asked Colin.

The shaggy brows of the Grand Odlum lifted, and he smiled. "Brother John . . . yes, I remember him. It was spring that year, too, and he loved a girl who had refused him. A very promising young man, but he had not lost enough."

"Not lost enough?" repeated Colin, puzzled.

"This journey," said the Grand Odlum simply, "is a long journey, and a hard one. Only those who have lost everything undertake it."

Startled, Colin said softly, "I've lost everything that matters to me."

"It happens," said the Grand Odlum, nodding.

"I've lost my future, the past hurts too much to think of, and I can't bear the present. I confess I do not like myself any more at all, and life even less, and certainly my thoughts are ugly companions to me now."

"It happens," said the Grand Odlum sympathetically.

"If I should enter your maze, would all this be changed?"

"Everything," said the Grand Odlum, "would be up to you."

"But would I learn why there is so much misery in the world, and why happiness is something that is only dangled and then snatched away?"

"Everything," said the Grand Odlum, "would be up to you."

Colin said angrily, "You're not very helpful, are you? Down in the village they advertise journeys into the next country and they speak of wondrous things there, of cities filled with people and jugglers and wild animals in cages. Your maze seems to offer nothing."

"Only hardship," said the Grand Odlum cheerfully. "Hardship and danger, too, and many doubts, and at the end—if you reach the end—a glimpse, perhaps, of the knowledge you seek. But only perhaps. The maze is not for everyone, you see, and it promises no ease. But it's you who came to me, Colin, not I to you." He stood up. "My time is valuable, and this is your decision, not mine." He shrugged. "It's a journey, that's all, and one that few people care to take or dare to take."

Colin was silent, and then he said resignedly, "You give no promises at all, and no reassurances."

"None."

Colin nodded. "I have thought, deep inside of

me, from something Brother John said, that it might be like this. And it's true—it's I who came to you, driven by need." He lifted his head and looked at the Grand Odlum silhouetted against the sky, his long beard silver in the sunlight. "I have known I would go," he said simply. "I have known it in the deepest part of me. It is a long journey?"

"There is no time inside the maze."

Colin nodded. "I have brought ten pieces of gold with me, a few clothes, some food, and my slingshot. This is enough?"

"It is enough."

Colin stood up, straightening his shoulders and lifting his chin. "Then I choose to go."

"You are quite sure?"

"I'm sure."

The Grand Odlum's face gentled. "Then I will take you to the door of the maze now."

"Yes," said Colin, and gathered up his few things.

"You had better take with you the saddle blanket," suggested the Grand Odlum. "Your horse will know the way home?"

"Yes." Colin unstrapped the blanket from Black Prince and tied it like a knapsack across his own shoulders. Then to Black Prince he whispered, "I love you, my friend, but the time has come for us to part." Stepping back a pace he shouted, "Go home, Black Prince," and gave the horse a slap on its flanks. The horse threw up his head and whinnied, and then galloped away into the woods.

2

The Grand Odlum led the way into the castle, stepping carefully around and over fallen rocks. Inside, in the vast Great Hall, portions of the roof had plunged to the ground, and the late afternoon sunlight sent shafts of gold across their path. They walked through marvelous arched rooms where the ruins of old tapestries still hung in shreds from the walls, and the only other sign of life was a mouse that scurried into a hole. At last the Grand Odlum opened a pair of huge oak doors, and they began going down, down, down. The steps were stone, worn smooth from age, and the windows were narrow slits in the wall; but there was a railing, and Colin clung to it. At the bottom of this staircase the Grand Odlum took a lamp from the wall and lighted it, for now they had descended too deeply into the earth for windows. The lantern's glow illuminated an endless narrow corridor laced with cobwebs that trembled a little as they passed.

And then suddenly they reached a small room, and the Grand Odlum, entering, stopped and held up the lamp. Following him Colin saw four walls on which strange designs and shapes had been drawn in brilliant colors. At the far end of the room stood a door, a very narrow iron door with two heavy bars across it.

"We are in the heart of the castle now," said the Grand Odlum, "and there is the door to the maze."

It was cold down here and Colin shivered. "I think," he said, hoping his voice didn't tremble, "that I will put on the sweater I brought with me." He put down his bundle and untied it, darting quick, sidelong glances at the drawings around him of spirals, snakes, and flowers, and at the door through which he would soon walk, leaving behind the Grand Odlum and everything familiar.

The Grand Odlum, watching him, said gently, "You're very young, Colin. It's not too late to turn back, you know. The door to the maze is still barred."

Colin thought about this as he pulled his sweater over his shoulders. He rewrapped his bundle carefully, tied it, and shook his head. "I would like to turn back," he admitted, "but something inside of me tells me I have to take this journey."

"It happens like that sometimes," said the Grand Odlum, nodding. "You're ready, then?"

"Yes."

The Grand Odlum lifted the first bolt from the door, and then he stopped and turned. He said fiercely, "I am not supposed to give counsel, Colin, but if search you must, let me give you this advice: The important thing is to carry the sun with you, inside of you at every moment, against the darkness."

"Darkness?"

"Yes, for there can be—will be—a great and terrifying darkness." With this he withdrew the second bar and flung the door open wide. "And there you are," he said, stepping back.

"Then good-bye, Grand Odlum," said Colin, "and thank you."

As Colin passed through the door the magician called after him, "And the name of my country is Galt."

With these words the door closed; Colin heard the clang of the first bolt and then of the second one as each was returned to its slot, barring entrance back into the castle. For a moment Colin stood listening, and then he looked around him, resolutely putting behind him the sound of the bolts being drawn, to replace them in his thoughts with the word "Galt."

He was in the maze, facing a very high stone

wall with a passage to the left and one to the right. A strange light came from overhead, certainly not from any sun because, surprisingly, it left no shadows; it was simply illumination, very pale and gray like the first light of dawn before the sun slips over the horizon. Colin decided to go to the right, for no reason except that he was right-handed, and swinging his two bundles from one hand, the blanket strapped across his shoulders, he set off down the path, whistling to keep up his spirits.

At home, he thought, Huldah would be adding wood to the great stove on which she cooked dinner and Lahvo would be bringing in the cows from pasture, their bells tinkling in the still clear air. "Well," he thought, "I have a dinner to eat, too. I'll walk for an hour and then stop and rest."

But it was difficult to judge an hour of time when there was no sun moving across the sky and no change in the light at all. After turning to the right in the beginning he decided that he would continue turning to the right every time he met with choice, and this he did, but at the first turn he soon found himself blocked by a stone wall and had to go back and start again.

He next chose a path to the left, but after walking for what felt like a very long time he was again brought to a halt by a stone wall. It was very frustrating. He returned and this time contin-

ued straight ahead until—faced with two paths—
he continued straight, and after walking almost a
mile found himself blocked once more by a wall.

Dazed and a little frightened now, Colin re-
traced his steps to the last intersection and sat
down to eat his dinner. He carefully unwrapped
his bundle, drank some lemonade and then a little
tea, and took a huge bite out of the roast beef that
Huldah had placed between two slices of home-
made bread. He began to feel better. He began to
wonder what shape this maze was, whether it was
square or round or oval like a bird's egg. He
thought suddenly, "But there are no birds here!"
and he was astonished that he'd not noticed something so important missing from the maze. He was
accustomed to drawing the birds he saw—it was
why he'd brought his colored chalk with him—but
there were neither trees nor flowers nor birds singing nor any sounds at all, only this dim and silent
twilight. He remembered that he'd thought there
would be no problem at all in getting through the
maze. He'd assumed that he would make short
work of it and that once he found the exit he'd be
in Galt, the country from which the Grand Odlum
came, which would be full of magicians who
would share their wisdom. He looked now at his
confidence and found it a small and shrunken
thing. He would have to do much better than this!

But the chalk gave him an idea. If many wrong turnings lay ahead of him he could at least mark each dead-end path so that he needn't repeat his mistakes over and over; he could also eat lightly to make his food last longer. With these decisions made, some of his confidence returned.

"What a poor traveler I am, growing discouraged so quickly," he thought. "After all, the Grand Odlum told me Galt wouldn't be easy to reach."

He set out again. At one point he traveled in a very long curve that returned him to the place he'd started from, but this time his chalk marks guided him quickly away to another part of the maze, and he began to feel that he might be making progress at last.

But as he grew tired a terrible sense of aloneness began to close in on him. It seemed as though a long time had passed since he'd talked with the Grand Odlum, and he wondered when he would see another human being again; in fact, he thought that with any encouragement he would like to sit down and cry. The stone walls on either side of him felt never-ending now and suffocating. He wondered if he was doomed to forever wander in this horrid maze, and thoughts of home came back to him: the look of his room when he went to bed at night, the feel of cool sheets, and the breeze blowing through the window. There was no wind here, just as there was no night or day. There was only emptiness, inside of him as well as all around him.

Tired out and nearly sick with longings, Colin unstrapped his blanket, rolled himself into it, and fell into a deep sleep.

He was awakened some hours later by the sound of voices.

He sat up straight, listening in amazement. There had been no voices before and they were still far away, but they rose and fell in a tide of conversation. The sound was that of a number of people, surely a dozen or more, talking, interrupting, calling to each other. Perhaps it had been night for these people when he had lain down to sleep, and now it was their morning and they were awake.

"People," he said out loud, and was startled by the sound of his own voice. "People to talk to —wonderful!" and then he shouted, *"Wonderful!"* The voices abruptly stopped, as if he'd been heard, and when they began again it was with startled exclamations. He was sure now they'd heard him. He jumped to his feet, rolled up his blanket, and eagerly set out to find companions.

It took him a long time. The murmur of voices guided him, but always there came those turnings when he found a stone wall blocking his path and had to go back and start again. It was perhaps two hours before he heard the voices clearly. He made one last turn and came to an excited, joyful stop.

He had entered what must be the very center of the maze, for here the walls fell back, leaving a huge and grassy square in which a group of people stood, sat, or strolled about. But there was more green here than just the grass, for all along the walls stood rows of tall green stalks bearing a round, grayish green fruit and gray blossoms so thick they nearly obscured the walls. The people had not seen him yet. Colin shouted, "I'm here, I found you!" and then, stepping forward, "I'm so glad to see you, I can't tell you how glad. I'm Colin."

Faces turned to stare at him. Eyes moved hungrily to the bright blue-and-white sweater he wore, and then to the scarlet of the blanket strapped to his back; he understood why when he saw that everyone here was dressed in gray or that whatever clothes they'd once worn had been bleached to the same color as the light in the maze. Their faces, too, had a curious grayish green tinge.

One of the men separated himself from the others and came toward him, saying in a gentle voice, "I'm Jeremy. Welcome, Colin, to the Wos. You must be very tired."

At once the others came to life, smiling at

him shyly, moving toward him and touching his clothes, while a plump, motherly woman placed her arms around him and said sadly, "Poor boy, poor boy."

It seemed a rather strange welcome, but Colin let himself be embraced and even gave the woman a reassuring smile when he saw there were tears in her eyes.

"How long have you been in the maze?" asked someone.

"Not long," he told them.

"Not long!" they echoed, and a woman turned to Jeremy and said, "He doesn't know, then, he doesn't know, poor lad."

"Know what?" asked Colin.

They looked at him with sad faces, and he stared back at them wonderingly. "Know what?" he demanded.

"That there isn't any way out."

Colin felt a chill grip him. "What do you mean?"

Jeremy came and stood beside him and patted his shoulder. "There is no exit from the maze."

The chill in Colin moved down to his stomach, and for a moment he thought he was going to be sick. "Nonsense," he said. "There has to be."

The plump woman shook her head. "You've been cheated like the rest of us, it's just the way everything else is in life. *There isn't any way out.*"

Colin said sharply, "I don't believe you, you can't have looked properly."

"Oh yes we have," Jeremy told him. "Some of us have been here for what must be a whole year now, and we've looked and looked. We've sent out expeditions day after day, using a rope and string unraveled from our clothes to find our way back. We've mapped and charted every path in the maze, right back to the castle door."

"But the Grand Odlum said—"

"Lies, all lies," cried one of the women. "He betrayed you, don't you see?"

Colin stubbornly shook his head. "I refuse to believe that."

"Well, you'll have to," she retorted angrily, "because there's just no exit. We're all stuck here —absolutely stuck."

"Now, now, Julia," crooned the motherly woman, "these shocks come hard, we all know that, and this one's just as unfair as the sorrows that brought us here." Turning to Colin she said, "My name is Maude."

"How do you do," said Colin politely.

"Jeremy can show you the maps and charts later," she told him, "and prove to you there's no way out, but in the meantime we're going to eat. Come and join us."

"Eat?" asked Colin, puzzled. "What do you eat here?"

"The fruit growing by the wall," she explained. "It's very nourishing, full of vitamins and proteins and juice, as well as pulp, so we're well provided for, anyway. How are we having it this morning, Michael?"

Michael, carrying a platter of fruit toward them, said, "Salted."

Maude nodded. "Sometimes we have it sugared," she confided to Colin, "but we're getting low on sugar. Salted's good, too. Have one."

Colin looked at the offered fruit and then at the faces of the others as they helped themselves. He said bluntly, "I don't think it can be all that great when it's turned your faces green."

Maude gave him a cold and reproachful glance. "If you're going to sulk and be spiteful and nasty—"

"That's how I feel," Colin said.

"Well, you'd better stop or we won't ask you to tell us what brought you to the maze. We want to give you our sympathy," she said. "We've all had terrible things happen to us, so you can talk very freely to us because we understand. After we learn what losses *you've* had you'll be grouped."

"Grouped?"

She nodded. "Yes, we're all grouped according to how much we've suffered. Jeremy's suffered the most of any of us, so he's the leader of all our groups just now. We each have a song about what's happened to us, and we'll make up a song for you, too. Today's my turn. You'll see. It's nearly time to begin."

"Begin what?" asked Colin.

"The chants and blessings." She held out a round green fruit to him with a smile. "Go ahead, it's good."

Colin sighed and gave in to it; he took a bite and found that it had the firmness of an avocado and the taste of a banana, but he took no more than the one bite.

"It's time now, Maude," said Jeremy, quietly joining them and carrying a guitar. To Colin he said, "After Maude has finished her song we'll want to give you a rousing welcome and hear all about you."

A hush fell over the square now as Maude walked to its center and the others gathered in a circle around her, their faces attentive and serious. Jeremy struck a chord on his guitar, and with a special smile for Colin, Maude began her song.

> I remember parents deadly as blight
> (so miserly, harsh, and angry could they be).
> But what I remember most each night
> is my first love, James, betraying me.

Here, to Colin's surprise, Maude stopped and the others broke in. "Oh woe," they chanted, "life is only a vale of tears, and what did we do to deserve this?"

Maude continued:

Oh the secrets of life are all concealed,
and search as we may they're never revealed.
For love of James I went mad with grief,
and out of despair married Tom, with whom joy was brief.

"Oh woe," chanted the chorus, "nothing turns out well, and what did we do to deserve this?"

The sad words and the dirge-like sound of the chants brought a terrible despair to Colin's heart; he discovered there were tears in his eyes.

Maude sang.

For a man twenty years older than I
was scarcely a mate,
With daughters full-grown and filled
with hate . . .

"Oh woe, oh woe," chanted her audience.

Two sons I bore, my life, my pride,
but one took sick with fever and died,
and the other ran away, and hence
I can speak of loss with eloquence.

"Oh life is only a vale of tears," came the chant, "and what did we do to deserve this?"

Colin stirred uneasily, feeling a touch of impatience now. He thought, "I feel worse here than

I did at home—and they want to make a song for me, too, like this?" He remembered back to the Grand Odlum's words and to his saying that it was a long journey, and a hard one. He recalled, too, the last words that the Grand Odlum had spoken to him: Almost against his will he had called after him, "And the name of my country is Galt."

This was not Galt. It couldn't be.

"This has to be only the beginning of the journey," he thought. "There *has* to be a way out of the maze—there has to be. *Somehow.*"

Maude sang:

So I came to the maze, wanting to learn and know,
only to meet here the most bitter blow.
No way out, no exit, dead end,
No more hope to nurture and tend.

"Oh woe," chanted her chorus, "the bitterest blow of all."

Yet here—oh miracle at last—is caring,
for the blows of life have made us sharing.
We walk together and we know . . . ah yes we know . . .

"That life is only a vale of tears," chanted the others. "Oh woe, oh woe . . ."

With one last chord from Jeremy's guitar the song ended, followed by a deep stillness and now and then a few sighs. Colin looked at his companions, at their gray faces and gray clothes and melancholy faces, and he felt a deep anger. He thought, "They can't have tried hard enough." His eyes wandered beyond them to the hideous gray fruit lining the walls, and then his glance moved to the top of the wall.

Maude, with a little bow, turned graciously to Colin. "Now you must tell us what tragedies brought *you* to the maze to join us."

But Colin said instead, thoughtfully, "Has anyone ever tried climbing to the top of that wall to look for a way out of the maze?"

Behind him Jeremy laughed. "To the top of the wall! Why, the walls are as tall as a house, thirty feet above us, at least."

Colin nodded. "But every person here is at least five feet tall," he pointed out, "and there are nine of you. By standing on each other's shoulders someone could reach the top of the wall and look around."

Maude glanced at Jeremy in alarm. "He's mad, isn't he?"

Jeremy smiled forgivingly. "Only very young, Maude. He doesn't believe us yet, you see."

"Well," Colin said stubbornly, "if you persuaded the others to form a human ladder—and some of those branches look strong enough to hang onto—what about me climbing to the top of the wall to look?"

"But there is no *exit*," Maude told him crossly.

"Somehow it might have been missed," pointed out Colin politely, and he turned to Jeremy. "Is there any reason not to try?"

Jeremy shrugged. "Not if it convinces you there's no way out."

"But we're interrupting our chanting hour," cried Maude, "and I haven't received the Ode of Pity and the Sympathy Blessing yet."

"It needn't take long," Jeremy said, giving Colin a hostile glance. "He'll see for himself soon enough, and then we can all settle down again."

"I felt his restlessness," Julia said disapprovingly.

"Exactly. Michael, Laslo, Peter—" He called the others one by one, and they gathered in a circle while he explained what they were to do and why.

One of the women sighed. "I'd forgotten how tiresome people from the outside world can be. They're all so full of optimism."

Laslo said gently, "But none of us believed there was no exit when we first came. We all had to be shown . . . and no one has thought of climbing the wall before."

"Well, let's get it done with, then," said Maude peevishly. "How do we begin?"

"The men first, because they'll have to bear the most weight," counseled Jeremy, and he began sorting them all by size. "Laslo, you're tallest and strongest, you stand there against the wall and I'll climb on your shoulders, followed by Peter, Michael, Jacob, and after that Maude and Julia and Johanna, then Catherine and the boy last of all."

The men took their places, but it became skittish work as the human ladder grew higher; there were humorous groans as the women climbed over the men, digging in their heels, and everyone held tight to a branch or two of the flowering stalks. But the chain held, and no one fell back. It was even possible, thought Colin, hearing one of the women laugh, that they were enjoying this.

At last Catherine called down, "I'm holding onto the top of the wall now. Send the boy up."

With a rope around his waist and trailing down behind him, Colin began his climb from shoulder to shoulder, very slowly, so as not to hurt anyone, until suddenly he stepped from the last pair of shoulders onto the top of the wall. "I'm here," he shouted, and turned to look around him, gasping at what he saw.

From this height the walls of the maze stretched out like a giant honeycomb a mile or more on all sides of him. But beyond the maze, far away, he could see blue sky and clouds racing across that sky; he could even feel a breeze on his face up here. Excitedly he turned to pull Catherine up behind him, and then the two of them extended the rope to Johanna, who tied it around her waist and was lifted to the top, after which they brought up the others, one by one, until they all stood on the wall.

"Blue sky," marveled Peter. "Look, did you ever see such blue?"

"And feel the breeze!" cried Catherine, touching her face in wonder. "I'd forgotten how it feels like silk!"

Jeremy had brought with him a stalk of the green fruit, which he planted like a flag between the cracks in the stones. "So we can find our way back," he told them.

"Back?" repeated Colin, filling his eyes with the blueness of the distant sky.

"Of course," said Jeremy with a look around him. "You don't see any exit yet from the maze, do you?"

"But we're on top of its wall," pointed out Colin. "Do let's walk around it," he told the others, and they eagerly followed him, edging their way carefully at first and not looking down.

But the wall was broad enough for walking. Colin led the way outward, away from the maze's center, and now when he glanced below he felt his heart constrict at the narrowness of the paths they'd walked. It was strange to be on top of the maze and look down into it. The others must have felt it, too, for he heard whispers and murmurs of surprise and awe behind him. They walked in single file, turning corners that drew them closer and closer to the far edge of the maze, and as they drew nearer to it, the country that lay beyond gradually became visible. Colin could see a desert of sand with tufts and patches of green here and there, stretching flat as a carpet up to a wall of towering, jagged cliffs. Beyond this, far, far away, his eye met with a line of snowcapped blue mountains.

It was not so promising a land to see, but Colin's heart lifted with joy because the Grand Odlum had not lied. There really was another country.

"Well," he said proudly, bringing them to the very edge of the maze, "here we are." And he looked down—way down—to the dunes of sand below.

Jeremy, turning his back on this, pointed to the honeycomb of walls over which they'd walked. "As you can see," he said sternly, "I was right. There's no exit from the maze, and there never was."

Colin stared at him in astonishment. "But we can leave it simply by jumping down from the wall!"

There was a gasp of shock from the others when he said this, and he felt them looking at each other questioningly.

Maude said crossly, "There should be an exit *inside* the maze."

"Exactly," said Jeremy. "We were told there'd be a proper exit, and inside is where an exit belongs."

Colin, ignoring this, said, "It's not a long jump, and the sand will make for a soft landing. Together we can manage anything. Who wants to jump first with me?"

Michael shook his head. "Not me," he said firmly. "I don't see any green fruit down there. I don't see anything that could feed us at all."

There was a hush following these words, and an uneasiness among them.

"Nor I," said Peter with a shiver. "That's a long walk to those cliffs, and then what? Look at the snow on those mountains beyond. Cold! Snow, and bitter cold."

"Well, I've no intention of going," said Maude in a loud voice. "I've not received my Sympathy Blessing yet."

Colin felt his excitement fade. He looked at her and then at Laslo. "And you?" he asked quietly.

Laslo sighed. "If only there was an exit *in* the maze I'd have more faith. It looks a hard land to travel in, lad, and who's to say what lies out there? Wild beasts, hunger, heat, cold. It'd be like jumping off a cliff blindfolded, with no guarantees at all. At least we know what's here behind us."

Colin felt a clutch of terror as he realized the implications of what they said. He cried out to them, "But you wanted to get out of the maze, and here is the way out—not through it, or around it, but *over* it! You wanted the exit, you said you searched for a long, long time! The maze has to be a trick to test us, don't you see that?"

He looked at them, but he could not find a pair of eyes willing to meet his own. They were all staring elsewhere—at their feet, at the horizon— not looking at him, their faces closed to him now.

"I don't understand," he pleaded. "Do you *like* the grayness back in the maze, and nothing but gray fruit to eat, and no sun and no wind? Won't anyone come?"

There was only silence, and then Maude said, "It's time for the odes and the blessings," and she turned away.

They all turned away now and began shuffling slowly along the wall, not looking back but leaving Colin there by himself.

He hesitated, panic rising in him at the thought of being alone again just when he'd found people. His panic was a terrible feeling. He did not want to go on by himself; he had tasted loneliness before he met the Wos and it had frightened him. A part of him wanted to go with them, wanted to shout, "Stop—wait for me," until he remembered the gray twilight in the maze and the chants and the sad songs. He gazed out at the blue sky and understood that he must decide quickly what he would do.

He did not make his choice willingly, and he did not make it happily. He made it out of desperation that he might give in to the fear that he felt.

He closed his eyes, leaned forward, and jumped.

3

It was a long fall, but Colin remembered to keep his knees bent, as he'd learned to do when jumping from a hay rick; even so he landed clumsily. Hitting the sand, he rolled over and over and over, then lay a minute catching his breath before he stood up, brushed the sand from his clothes, and pulled off the heavy sweater he wore because already he could feel the heat pushing at him.

Only then did he look up at the wall, hoping still to see one of the Wos standing there, but no one had come back, not even to see if he had survived his jump. Sadly he turned his back to it and looked at what lay ahead.

Laslo had been right; it was a forbidding scene: just sand and heat and that distant wall of high cliffs; no shade and perhaps no water. Still in the shadow of the wall Colin drew out half a sandwich and ate it, then drank a little cold tea.

By eating sparingly he thought he might have food enough for two more days, and enough drink for one. But he would have to be very careful.

With a last glance at the wall behind him he set out to cross the desert, feeling very small under the huge sky, and very insignificant.

A lizard crossed his path. Once he saw a jackrabbit and called out to him, but the animal only gave him a startled glance and fled. The sand was so hot underfoot that soon Colin removed his boots and carried them until the sand so scorched his feet that he had to draw them on again. As he walked, the cliffs ahead shimmered in the heat, sometimes moving toward him, then receding, shrinking and expanding like shapes in a dream.

His thoughts grew sad. He began to remember the Wos now with sympathy; he even started wondering what his own sad song would have been if he'd stayed, and he decided that he could have been happy with them because anything would be kinder than this. He would at least have had sympathy and a sense of family again. He became racked with doubts about his decision to jump from the wall.

He sipped a little lemonade and went on.

He grew tired—the blanket on his back was hot and heavy, and his two small bundles, of clothes and food, were burdensome.

His misery deepened. There was no shade,

only a grinding heat and a brightness that hurt his eyes.

But at least there promised to be night in this land, for after hours of walking the sky began to dull and the sun to withdraw some of its searing, scorching heat. The cliff had grown steadily closer until now he could see the seams in its rock—only a few miles away, he guessed, but close enough to bring a fresh worry to him: How on earth was he going to climb the sheer sides of such a cliff? Walls, he thought—walls everywhere!

But this problem would have to wait for a new day, he decided, and with night coming he began to look for shelter, knowing that if the sand had been excruciatingly hot by day it could be equally as cold at night. Off to his right he saw a strange collection of boulders thrust into a pile, as if a giant had tossed them there, and he headed toward them. When he reached the outermost rock he sat down in its shade and for only the third time since leaving home unwrapped his parcel of food. He had just taken a sip of tea when a voice behind him whispered, "Water? You have water?"

Colin leaped to his feet and spun around. Several feet above him the face of a young man peered down from the top of the rock. Colin gasped, "Who—what—" and then he saw how the young man's face was blistered from the sun, and his lips swollen. Hastily he climbed up the rocks, knelt beside the stranger, and lifted the flask of tea to his lips.

The young man was so weak that his head had to be held, but when he'd drunk from the flask he gave a long, blissful sigh. "*Urgan dap*," he murmured. "Thank you." He closed his eyes and then opened them. "But you're a miracle," he said hoarsely, staring up at Colin. "No one walks in the desert by day. Who are you?"

"I'm Colin, but if no one walks in the desert by day, what are *you* doing here?"

The young man's face was terribly burned, the skin peeling from it in long strips, and his lips were cracked; he must have been many days in the heat. He wore a tunic bleached by the sun into a faded scarlet, with strange black designs on it. He was young, surely no more than a few years older than Colin, just old enough to have a dark stubble of beard at his chin.

"I was put here to die," the young man said. "Banished."

"*Put* here? Brought here?" Colin said blankly, and looked around in amazement. "By whom? Where are the people who did such a thing?"

The stranger tried to speak again, but only rasping sounds came from his throat; Colin leaned over and gave him a few more sips of tea. "What's your name?"

"Zan," he said, and with difficulty pulled himself up to a sitting position. Lifting one arm, he pointed out at the desert, and beyond it to the wall of rock. "That cliff . . . is not a true cliff," he told Colin, "but hollow inside . . . with many rooms. It's the kingdom of the Talmars." Slumping back, he gasped, "I've no strength. Have you food as well?"

"Yes, I've food," said Colin, and drew out his bread. Because of Zan's swollen lips he soaked small pieces of the bread in tea, and fed them to him one by one. As he did this the sun touched the desert's horizon and stained it crimson, then slid away, trailing behind it brilliant streamers of saffron, purple, and lemon yellow.

"Mmm," murmured Zan at last, with a shake of his head. "Not too much at once. It is your food, too, which is life itself in the desert. I thank you for it."

"You would do the same for me."

"Would I?" asked Zan wonderingly. "There is not much kindness among us Talmars."

Colin said bluntly, "No, not if they left you out here to die of heat and hunger. How could such a thing happen?"

With the disappearance of the sun Zan had begun to shiver. Colin unstrapped his blanket and placed it over him. "It's big enough for the two of us," he said, "but I'm not ready yet for sleep. Can you talk?"

"I think now, yes," said Zan, and began slowly, haltingly, to speak of the Talmars.

There had not always been a city inside the cliff, said Zan. According to the old myths and legends, the people had come from a far place, through some kind of labyrinth or maze.

"A maze!" exclaimed Colin in wonder.

"Yes, and they endured a great deal," added Zan. There had been a sandstorm in which two of their thirteen people were lost. In those days a cave existed at the base of the cliff, and inside it a spring of good water; finding this at last, the eleven survivors of the storm took refuge. The next day four of the members of the party insisted on continuing the journey despite the losses and the hardship ahead of scaling the cliff. Their leader, Talmar, had argued with them and had set up guards to prevent their going, but during the second night the four people slipped away.

Zan was silent a minute, and then he said, "I think that's when the trouble began, the hatred and the cruelty. A week ago I would have told you our history the way it's written in our records, but there is nothing like facing death," he said with a wry smile, "to change how one sees things. The four who went away are called in our stories the Contemptibles, but now I ask myself why they should be called Contemptibles for wanting to finish the journey that all of them had set out to make. They must have found a way over the cliff, too, because it is said they were hunted a long time. Not even their bones were discovered, which has to mean they succeeded, don't you think?"

"I wonder how," mused Colin, staring at the cliff.

"I think their success must have excited the others, and perhaps they begged Talmar to leave, too, which is when Talmar changed from leader to ruler."

"He said no?"

Zan nodded. "He forbade them to go. He told them everything they needed was here, and he set them to work expanding the cave, using only stones to chip away the rock. It's said that they worked every day from sunrise to sunset, except for their hunting days, when they tracked animals for food or captured the wild desert horses to breed. Those people who stayed are called the Great Ones, the founders of the kingdom," said Zan, "but I think now that Talmar simply turned them into slaves."

Colin gazed somberly out across the sand at the cliff wall, trying to imagine it alive with people inside. "Why did they bring you here to die?" he asked.

Zan sat up, his back against a rock, the blanket around his shoulders. He said quietly, "My uncle is King Talmar the Eighth, and I did not obey the First Rule of Xemplary."

"And what rule is that?"

"Never to speak against the King."

"But what did you say of him?"

"What I said was admitted to my friends, five of them, and in secret. Together we whispered of his greed and his cruelty, not knowing there was a spy hole in the room, and an eavesdropper listening."

"And for that you were given—this?" Colin said in dismay.

"No," said Zan with a shake of his head. "I was first ordered to kill my friends one by one, according to the Rules of Xemplary, which meant the first one by strangulation, the second by stabbing, the next by poison, the fourth by smothering, and the last by decapitation. When I refused to do such a thing, my friends were sentenced to imprisonment and torture, and for me the punishment was slow death in the desert."

Shaken by this, Colin said in a shocked voice, "Your King of Talmar is indeed cruel—you are right in that, certainly!"

"All our kings have been cruel," said Zan sadly, "and the people grow more and more frightened and hopeless." His glance moved beyond

Colin and his eyes widened. "Heavenly Zircon, they've seen you!" he gasped. "Spies must have been watching all this time!"

Colin's gaze followed Zan's and he stiffened. Where before there had been an unchanging smooth surface in the cliff there was now a dark square, an opening in the facade near the base of the cliff from which several men on horses were emerging into the desert's fading light.

"They've seen you!" Zan cried in horror. "Oh, Colin, can you run fast, can you go back from wherever you came? They'll whip or kill or imprison you for sharing bread with me. For speaking to me. For being here."

Colin's eyes were on the men astride the horses; he could see now that their tunics were a blazing scarlet, as Zan's must have been once, and that they were galloping toward the circle of rocks on which he and Zan sat. He said quietly, "It's too late, Zan, there's nowhere to hide or flee. Besides, to continue my journey I have to find a way through your kingdom. It appears I would have to meet them sometime."

"You don't know what you're saying," cried Zan. "You don't want to meet the Talmars. They'll kill you!"

Colin made no answer but leaned over his knapsack, brought out his slingshot, and tucked a handful of smooth round stones into his pocket.

He watched the horsemen approach—there were only three of them—and as they drew near he stood up to meet them. In the twilight it was difficult to see their eyes, but he saw the hardness of their faces, two of them bearded, and he knew he mustn't betray his fear, which was very real after what Zan had told him of the Talmars.

He stood unmoving as they reined in just below him.

"You are blaspheming," called out their leader angrily. "You're consorting with a banished citizen of Talmar. Who are you? Where do you come from?"

"I have been speaking with Zan, nephew of King Talmar the Eighth," Colin said boldly.

"He is no one and nothing," the man shouted. "Who are you?"

"I am a stranger, come to this land through the maze."

"The maze!" exclaimed one of them, and the words provoked a startled murmuring among them.

"And I demand to see your king," he added.

"Oh, you'll see him, all right! Come down from the rock."

"Not alone," Colin told him. "Zan has to come as well."

Behind him Zan whispered, "*No!* They'll kill you for that! Leave me here and go."

Colin shook his head and stood very still, waiting, and as he waited the last vivid colors disappeared from the horizon, leaving only the faintest glow of light.

The men spoke among themselves, and then two of them dismounted and moved toward the rock, one to approach it from the right, and the other from the left. Colin lifted his sturdy slingshot, fitted a smooth stone to it, whispered a prayer to Hoveh, and taking aim sent his stone flying toward the man on the right. It struck him in the temple; before he had even met the ground a second stone was spinning toward the man on the left, who sank to his knees clutching his throat.

Colin said in a hard voice, "Zan comes with me."

The leader laughed but there was uneasiness in his voice. "You are tougher than you look. Bring the Contemptible along then. He can die in Talmar as quickly as here."

Colin helped Zan to his feet and guided him down from the rock to one of the horses. Boosting him into the saddle, he climbed up behind him, slingshot still in hand. He said, "We two will ride together; your friends can take the remaining horse."

"No friends of mine now," the man sneered.

"They're cowards and weaklings. Let them stay and die."

Colin shook his head. "In my country we take care of our people. Tie them to the second horse."

The man stared at him in astonishment; his face hardened and he turned away angrily.

"Heavenly Zircon!" whispered Zan, watching. "He's obeying you! *This* is something to see!"

When the two men, still unconscious, had been tied across the saddle of the empty horse, they set out through the dusk, riding side by side. They rode in silence for a mile or more, but as they neared the entrance to the cave wall, the leader turned his head and looked at Colin.

He said curtly, "You are more of a fool than I thought, to bring these two men with us." He added shrewdly, "And an even greater fool to neither wound nor kill me as well, for I have been witness, and I am Shang, captain of the King's Guards. You had the power to kill me back there. Are you such a fool you didn't see this?"

Colin gave him a long look in return. "I saw it," he said, "but I live by the rules of the country I come from, and there we try to live with honor."

"What's 'honor'?"

"We believe in kindness to one another, and we do not kill unless in war or self-defense."

Shang's glance was curious. "Are you a king's son to speak so boldly?"

"Everyone in my country speaks as I do."

"A country of weaklings, then," he said contemptuously as they approached the hole in the cliff.

"Perhaps," said Colin with a shrug, "but the entrance to the maze lies in my country; and if your people came through that maze long ago, then once they, too, lived by honor."

Shang's laugh was harsh. "Just see then," he pointed out, "where your honor has brought you. To the kingdom of Talmar and to captivity."

It was on these words that they rode through the door in the wall to enter the cliff kingdom.

4

At their entrance several guards sprang to their feet to release great chains that lowered a rock over the gap through which they'd entered; and Colin, looking back, marveled at the smoothness of the fit. Then his gaze turned to what lay ahead of them, to a tunnel lighted by torches and a dozen men in black-and-scarlet tunics riding toward them.

To one of the men Shang said curtly, "Here are two Contemptibles for your prison. My own men met with an accident. Take them to the Torture Room." With this he rode away.

Zan whispered, "We're in luck, Colin. He's not taking us to the King—not yet, at least—and he didn't remind the guards of who I am."

"We'll need something more than luck," murmured Colin as the guards surrounded them, one of the men reaching over to take the reins from his hands.

They were led in grim silence down a long ramp into the bowels of the cliff. It was a broad passage, with rooms opening from it on either side, and to Colin it was a thing of amazement that Zan had described it as being carved out of the rock by human hands. They passed other brightly lighted ramps leading upward to higher levels, but whenever they passed other human beings the people shrank back against the wall as if to make themselves invisible; they did not wear black-and-scarlet tunics, Colin noticed, but rough homespun, shabby and worn with age.

And then, gradually, Colin became aware of sounds ahead, a steady murmur like the drone of hundreds of bees, so intense that it puzzled him and made him uneasy. As they rode nearer, the mumble of sounds turned into moans and cries. The noise increased, becoming a babel until, meeting a wall, they turned abruptly to the right to face a pair of wide iron gates, and through these gates Colin looked into hell.

The sight turned him cold with horror.

A vast cavern lay before him, a huge room lighted by dozens of fires. Over one of the smaller fires near the gate a man was chained to a rod that slowly turned, carrying him into the fire and then away, over and over, his mouth and eyes alive with unheard screams.

Other men hung upside down over the fires,

suspended by ropes from the roof of the cave, their bodies dancing wildly to get away from the flames.

In the center a crazy kind of treadmill existed over which men walked unceasingly, because if they faltered for only a moment the moving platform would carry them into the flaming pit below. Around the cavern stood cells from which men watched, their faces terrified, as Colin's was now.

With an effort he steadied himself. The guard ordered the two of them to dismount. Zan, scarcely strong enough to stand, leaned on Colin while the gates were opened, and then limped next to him as the guards led them to the nearest cell. Once inside Zan clung to the bars, staring dazedly at the horrors around them.

"*No!*" shouted Colin above the noise, and pried Zan's hands from the bars and pulled him to a corner of the cell. "Don't look," he told Zan fiercely. "Not yet, not yet, it can only weaken you."

"But I see Aselph out there," he cried, "and Rolfe . . . my friends!"

"The important thing for now," Colin told him, "is that they've not searched me yet. I still have food and drink; we have to eat before the guards come back—and quickly."

"Eat?" cried Zan. "For what? Why?"

"For either life or death," Colin told him, and

unwrapping his packet of food he divided it and handed half to Zan. "Eat. Force it down."

They crouched in silence, concentrating on meat and bread while Colin stuffed cake and raisins into his pocket, and hid both his slingshot and one empty flask under his shirt. They were seen, however, before they finished. Colin heard Zan's sudden cry and turned just in time to roll out of the way as a long iron rod flew past him, hurled at such a deadly speed through the bars of the cell that when it struck the wall it buried itself between the stones and remained there, quivering. Two guards flung open the door to the cell and rushed in to snatch away the food. While one of them pulled the iron rod from the wall, the other gave Colin a blow that sent him sprawling unconscious across the cell floor.

In the blackness that followed, both Brother John and the Grand Odlum moved through Colin's dreams, and both seemed to speak to him but he could not hear their words; they vanished and suddenly he was running in the desert, and what he ran toward was a stream of water, a brook making wonderful musical sounds as it hurried over rocks and pebbles . . . When he opened his eyes at last it was with an awareness that a long time had passed and that something in particular had startled him back to consciousness. He found himself on the floor, staring at a huge flat rock that lay just beyond his fingertips, and behind it a wall with a gaping hole in it from which the stone had apparently fallen. But it was the cessation of noise that had awakened him; the shouting had stopped, and outside in the great cavern only a few groans could be heard.

He turned his head and saw Zan sitting with his back against the wall, eyes closed. At the turn of Colin's head Zan opened his eyes and said in a tired voice, "It seems they do not like to kill people too fast. They let them rest a few hours every day. I had hoped you were dead; it would have been kinder for you because our turn to be tortured comes next."

Colin scarcely heard him; he had dreamed of running water and he still heard the faint sound of running water, which left him wondering if he had gone mad. He shook his head to clear it but still he heard the faraway sound of water rushing over stones. He lifted himself and sat up, looking around him. The fires had been extinguished in the cavern outside, and the guards were kneeling in a circle near the gate tossing what looked to be dice. He said, "Water."

"There is none," replied Zan.

"No," said Colin, puzzled. "I hear water."

"They struck you hard indeed, then," said Zan, not moving.

Frowning, Colin looked around him, and then

he glanced at the stone, remembering how the long iron rod had embedded itself in the wall and had then been torn out. He looked at the hole from which it came and dragged himself closer to it. As he drew nearer the sound of running water grew more distinct. The hole in the wall was just a little larger than his head; he placed his head in it and realized that he wasn't mad, after all.

When he spoke his voice sounded strange, even to him. "Zan," he said.

"Mmmm?"

"Come over here."

"Why?"

"Come. Come now."

With a sigh Zan crawled toward him. "What is it?"

"Listen," said Colin, and pulled him close to the hole in the wall.

Zan turned an astonished face to Colin. "There's water down there."

"*Running* water," Colin pointed out. "Water that goes somewhere." He reached his arm through the hole and brought it back in triumph. "*And space between the walls for a person to drop down to it.*"

They stared at each for a long time, wide-eyed, not speaking, and then at the same moment each of them reached for the rock on the floor, and by pushing, pulling, and heaving they succeeded in propping it back in place over the hole before it could be seen by the guards. When this had been done they looked at each other again.

Zan said quietly, "It could go nowhere."

Colin nodded. "Very true."

"And we would be trapped."

"Yes," agreed Colin.

"My friends are out there," said Zan, gesturing toward the cavern.

Colin nodded. "As well as five guards, and I have only four stones left for my slingshot."

"But when the guards went out after hitting you they didn't bother to lock the door to our cell," Zan told him. "I saw this."

They smiled at each other, and Colin reached out and grasped Zan's hand. "We can at the very least try," he said. "Better this than to be roasted over a fire like an animal."

They turned and looked at the guards, who still had their heads together by the gate. Careful not to make any sudden movement, Colin inched his way to the door of the cell and glanced around the cavern. Men lay sprawled here and there, exhausted and torn. He said quietly to Zan, "They are weak, and so are you. It would be best if you slide out of the door when I do, and while I try to stun the guards you hurry among the prisoners and alert those who can walk."

Again they exchanged a long glance, as if to

acknowledge that this could be good-bye, that Colin's aim might be faulty, or that they might be discovered too early. Then Colin brought out his slingshot and the four remaining stones, and opening the cell door he slipped outside. Zan followed.

"O Hoveh," prayed Colin silently, fitting a stone to the slingshot, "these men are cruel only from ignorance. I do not wish to kill them, only to render them helpless for a little while. Make my aim straight and my hands steady."

The first stone hit a guard in the back of the neck and sent him sprawling among the dice. Before the other guards had recovered from their astonishment two more of them fell over, and then as the last two jumped to their feet Colin's fourth stone struck one of them between the eyes and he fell. This left one guard, who gave a great shout and roared toward Colin like an enraged bull.

But Zan was shouting now, too, and all over the cavern dazed men were picking themselves up —those who could stand—and limping toward him. Colin, facing the charging guard without weapons, resigned himself to death.

And then, only a few feet away from Colin, the guard in the scarlet tunic stopped in his tracks.

It was Shang, captain of the guards.

"You!" he growled, and lifted an arm to strike, then hesitated. "You," he cried again, and just as suddenly dropped his arm.

Colin said steadily, "There is more kindness in you than you realize." He gestured toward the wounded men whom Zan was herding into the cell. "We're escaping, Shang."

"There's no escaping from Talmar," said Shang harshly, and he added, "I'll have to sound the alarm." He looked behind Colin to the cell, his glance puzzled.

"Give us three minutes," pleaded Colin, and snatching up several boards of wood he turned toward the cell, seeing that Zan and those with him had pulled the stone from the wall. Once inside he turned and called to Shang warmly, "Thank you!"

Zan had assembled nine men to join them. "I've explained," he said, "and they have heard the water."

"Then we must go quickly, throwing down a board for each two men to keep them afloat." *If*, he added silently, *there is somewhere to go and we have not exchanged torture for drowning.* "Quickly, quickly!" he cried.

It was decided that he would go first because he was the strongest; if he survived he could help the others keep their heads above water. Without hesitating Colin pushed his legs through the hole in the wall, edged his body through, and let go. As he dropped into endless darkness he thought to himself, "I may soon grow accustomed to this jumping into the unknown," and he realized that he was almost smiling at the thought.

It felt a long way down, and the stone walls on either side were clammy with moisture, but their surfaces were lined with moss and lichen, which softened the bumps. The sound of the rushing stream turned into a roar and suddenly—so suddenly it took his breath away—Colin plunged into water and sank until his feet touched a rocky bottom. He surfaced in darkness, sputtering and gasping for breath, only to be seized by a strong current.

It was an unfair battle—he fought hard but he was carried away at once, struggling to keep his head above water, bumping into rocks too slippery to grasp, and spun in circles by whirlpools. There was no time to wonder what was happening to Zan or the others when every second his own life was in doubt. Over and over he was hurled—slammed into rocks, pulled away, sucked under and sped along through inky darkness—until, far ahead, he saw a thin ray of light reflected off a rock wall, and abruptly the rapids swept him around a curve and spewed him out into calmer waters. In that splinter of light coming from somewhere above Colin saw that he had emerged into an underground lake. Utterly exhausted, he swam to a ledge along the rock wall and dragged his body across it.

A moment later two others were swept into the lake and struggled to the ledge to lie gasping beside him. Another appeared, and then four more heads surfaced like corks bobbing in the water. Colin, rousing himself now, saw Zan emerge at last and helped him climb onto the ledge.

There were no more. Of the eleven of them only nine had made it.

They lay there exhausted except for Colin, who had recovered enough to sit up, his back against the wall. As he looked around him, he thought that Talmar might have been carved out of rock by its people, but long before they had arrived, Nature had done some carving of her own. This underground lake, and the opening to it by which they had entered, must have been created by the sheer force of water pushing its way through rock. But there must also be an exit for the water as well as an entrance, he thought, for otherwise the lake would overflow. When they had rested they would have to find it.

He slept, and when he awoke he saw that Zan was awake, too, and sitting up. Zan said, "We lost Aselph and Rudd, and they were good friends."

"I'm sorry."

"I have been thinking of them as I sit here, Colin, and I have also been thinking that this must be the way those four long-ago Contemptibles continued their journey."

Colin nodded. "That spring of water you mentioned at the base of the cliff."

"Yes."

"Do you think there may be Talmars who still know of this underground river?"

Zan said slowly, "It *could* be written in the sacred Xemplary records, which only the King sees." He suddenly smiled. "You will have to collect more stones then, my friend. That weapon of yours is powerful, and you do wondrous things with it. But we will all need weapons, if only sticks and stones." He sighed. "Of course this is supposing that we'll see daylight again."

Colin said, "If those four Contemptibles found a way, then we can, too. We have to look for the place where the water flows out." Gesturing toward their sleeping companions, he asked, "Do you know these men who escaped with us?"

Zan nodded. "They're all of them people who displeased the King. That man with white hair is Prince Kyte, in charge of assemblies, a very important job. The young man with red hair is Orlo, brother to Shang, captain of the guards. He refused to murder his best friend and was taken prisoner many weeks ago. I'm surprised he is still alive. Besides my friends Loman and Rolfe I know the others only by sight. They were accused of plotting rebellion against the kingdom and were imprisoned the day before I was."

"An unhappy kingdom," said Colin.

"Yes." He turned to the others and called out, "Prince Kyte, Orlo, Loman—wake up, we must go on."

Colin, patting his pockets, brought out water-logged cake and pressed the crumbs into tiny wet balls; these he passed around, as well as the raisins, which were swollen from their trip through the rapids but still intact. It was not enough, but it was something, and the men ate slowly, savoring every crumb.

"It is a miracle that we are alive," said the Prince when he'd finished. "Young as you are, stranger, our lives are yours. Command us."

Colin said humorously, "My first command, then, would be to get us out of here, but let me do the exploring because I've not been tortured, as you have. Save your strength and rest."

With this he stood up and, crouching low, began to make his way along the ledges and shelves of rock that encircled the lake. It was dark, and he stumbled often. He traced the solitary ray of light to a crack in the ceiling of the cave; but although its brilliance struck the dark water and reflected itself a dozen times, it was only a very tiny crack that produced the light. He could use it as guidance, though, depending upon it like the single ray of a lantern.

It did not take long for him to discover the outlet for the lake's water. Actually, he found two: one through a hole in the rocks, such as the one they had already passed through; the other a dry passageway pointing upward toward the earth's surface. He came back to tell the others.

"Which do you choose?" he asked.

"You give us choice?" said Loman, astonished.

"Of course. Let's take a vote on whether to continue by water or try the passage upward, since either will take us into new dangers."

"What's a 'vote'?" asked Zan.

"Each man says yes or no to these two possibilities. This is called a vote, and we obey the choice of the majority."

"Amazing," said Prince Kyte.

The vote was taken; the choice was to follow the waterless passage that led upward, because if they met with no exit they could still return and follow the stream.

Zan thought it might be morning when they set out; Colin believed it still to be night. In any case they moved slowly, resting often, because all of them except Colin were in pain, as well as weak from lack of food. They moved in darkness, holding fast to each other, and when their feet slipped on stones they collected the stones for Colin's slingshot, until his pockets were stuffed with them again.

After a long time a vague light began to filter into the passageway from somewhere ahead. The steepness of the path leveled out and the passage narrowed, becoming a tunnel so that they were forced to creep along, until—abruptly—they met with a tall and curious circle of stones that must certainly have been placed there by men. The stones formed a kind of round chimney in which a door had been left, and Colin, crawling inside and looking up, said, "I see light! This is the way out, it has to be!"

There was a murmur of awe from the men behind him.

"Is the opening large?" asked Zan.

"Wide enough—just barely—for a person to squeeze through," said Colin. "From here it looks as if two great rocks stand there, not quite touching, leaving a space between."

Again Colin went first, being the strongest, so that he could pull the others up and out. He emerged between two great rocks, unable to see beyond or around them, aware only of a strange red sky overhead, but whether it was sunrise or sunset he could not guess. His companions followed, one by one, and only when they were all out did they begin to look for footholds to help them climb over the rocks surrounding them.

It was Zan who first reached the top of a rock, and it was Zan, peering over it, who cried out in horror.

"What is it?" shouted Colin, and scrambled up the last few feet to his side.

There was no need for words. Those long-ago Talmars had recorded the existence of the underground stream, after all, and had passed it on from king to king.

Waiting for them just below were Talmars in bright red tunics, the guards standing two deep in a circle around the rocks, a line of soldiers on horseback behind them, and the crimson sky above them, like an omen of the blood that was about to be shed.

5

They had come out of the underground passage only a short distance from what was the main gate to the kingdom of Talmar. There were crowds of people standing at that gate, and more of them lined up along the wall that had been built to guard the gate. They were waiting there, thought Colin, to watch a massacre of nine prisoners who had sought to escape and now were surrounded and doomed. Bitterly he gazed down at the soldiers, while they—caught, too, in the surprise of the moment—stared back. Colin noted their hard faces and the sharpened metal rods they carried. He recognized Shang, captain of the guards, sitting astride a horse next to a man dressed differently from the others, a hard, arrogant, cruel-looking man, heavily bearded and wearing a black fur cape over his scarlet tunic.

In that moment a terrible rage came over Colin, building up in him until it shook him. He thought of how he had watched his mother and father die; he thought of his long and lonely trip across the desert, of the Talmars tortured like animals inside the cliff; he thought of their escape by the underground stream, of the two men lost in the rapids, and his rage was savage at their being found and trapped. He stood up and shook his fist at the men below. "You murderers of innocent people," he shouted. "Kill us if you must—go ahead, take us all, you men who torture from love of cruelty."

In his fury he screamed the words at them, and then he lifted his slingshot, notched a stone to it, and aimed it at the man in the black fur cape. The man pulled his horse to one side to escape the stone, lifted an arm, and shouted angry words to his men. At his command the guards raised their long pointed metal rods. From the direction of the gate came the sound of a horn blowing, and in a single moment a dozen rods flew through the air toward Colin. He ducked and one glanced off his shoulder, but he had already sent a second stone flying after the first, and then another. All around him the pointed rods were falling, striking the rocks with a metallic sound, and Zan was picking them up.

"Here, Prince Kyte," called Zan, tossing him a rod. "And Orlo—one for you."

As swiftly as the rods flew through the air

they were returned by the nine men on the rock, until the scene was thick with flying stones and rods, and men below began falling to the ground.

"We are wildly outnumbered," thought Colin, "but we can at least go down taking a few Talmars with us!" To Prince Kyte he shouted, "Watch the rear! They'll try to climb behind us!"

Disliking very much the man in the black fur cape, who still sat sneering on his horse and appeared to be in command, Colin notched a fresh stone to his slingshot and aimed at him again. This time the stone hit the man hard in his chest and knocked him from his horse. Instantly a horn blew, and the men below lowered their rods in surprise. Taking advantage of this lull, Colin sent another stone flying at the man in the fur cape so that it reached him as he stood dazed next to his horse. This stone hit him between the eyes, and he sank to the ground.

"Heavenly Zircon!" gasped Zan beside him. "That's the King you just hit—the King of Talmar!"

There was a great silence under the red sky as the soldiers realized who had fallen. It was an ominous silence. From the walls of the cliff a horn sounded again, and through the gates rode a veritable new army of soldiers. Colin's heart sank as he saw the number of red tunics marching toward them under that blood-red sky.

One of the guards, kneeling beside the man in the fur cape, cried out, "He's not wounded—he's *dead!*"

"The King—dead?"

"He's dead—they've killed him!"

The words were spoken in awe and fear, followed by uneasy murmurings and then silence, until Shang turned his horse and rode a few paces toward the gate. He shouted to the people, *"The King is dead—the King of Talmar is dead."*

When he had said this he turned and looked at Colin across the heads of his men, and the expression on his face was a strange one, not hostile but full of a meaning that Colin could not read. In any case Colin had little time for pondering it, for the column of soldiers was very near now, their metal rods flashing and ready.

"Well, friend," said Zan, moving closer. "It looks as if we are doomed now, but at least—"

A great roar suddenly came from the throats of the people lining the walls, and men and women began streaming out of the gate shouting and crying. As the soldiers turned in surprise to look, the people of Talmar began snatching up stones and pebbles. The first wave of people hurled these, not at the Contemptibles or at Colin, who had killed their king, but at the line of marching soldiers.

At this same moment Shang rode through the

men surrounding the rocks and reined in his horse. Looking up at Zan and Colin, he peeled off his red tunic and threw it to the ground. "My brother Orlo is up there," he called out. "Tell him his brother Shang wishes to fight with him."

"Let us go down!" cried Colin. "The people of Talmar are fighting *with* us! Hurry!"

And down they went, those of them strong enough to fight.

It was a mighty battle. It lasted for hours under the blood-red sky, as if the heavens themselves had known what the day would bring; and into the fight Colin poured all of his anger. His pent-up rage and grief were behind every blow that he struck, as if by fighting cruelty in this Talmar kingdom he was fighting every cruelty in the world. He was everywhere, sometimes pulling soldiers from their horses, at times crouching to notch a stone to his slingshot, but more often he was wrestling a guard or a soldier to the ground, biting, kicking, punching. His anger was unfaltering; he was like a cup filled with it to the brim.

And then, quite suddenly, a hush swept over the battlefield and Colin, glancing up, saw that all over the field the soldiers who weren't wounded were pulling off their red tunics in a gesture of surrender. Into this silence a voice called, "What kind of fools have we been to fight for a king we've hated!"

"A dead king now, too," growled a guard.

A soldier shouted angrily, "But who will be king next—tell us *that!* For the King's son is no better than Talmar the Eighth!"

"Let the prisoners speak!" shouted a woman. "It's because of them we're free. Round up the prisoners and let them speak!"

"Where is Zan, nephew to the King? And Orlo? And Prince Kyte—"

"And the strange one," called out Shang, "the one who says he came through the maze."

"The maze!" Again there were murmurs of astonishment at this word.

"You mean the young one who fought like a man possessed? There he is—over there."

Zan stepped forward out of the crowd and said, "He is my friend, and his name is Colin."

All over the field people began moving toward Colin, and he looked at them in surprise. He realized that because he was a stranger and because he had come through the maze they expected something of him, but he did not feel wise enough to give them anything. He did not even feel anger any more, he had spent it all. In its place a sense of peacefulness was filling him; and in this strange moment, when he had exhausted not only his body but his rage, he remembered the Grand Odlum and he wondered if his thought-forms might have changed a little now, those thought-forms that had kept the Grand Odlum from sitting too near him. This made him smile.

He met the Talmars smiling, and knew—it came to him suddenly—what he must do. He said, "I have no words to say, but I have something to show you and something all of you must see. Zan and I will lead the way. I beg of you to get horses for those who can't walk, and follow us."

"Heavenly Zircon! Follow us where?" asked Zan.

"We'll take them to the place we came from," Colin told him. "You know the way—show me."

They lined up slowly and set out for the gate to the kingdom, a procession of people old and young, with clothes torn and faces streaked with dust and blood. As they marched through the gates they were met with cheers from those too frail to fight, and they, too, joined the procession. Someone produced music, and then a song. Singing triumphantly, they marched through a great square and then down hallways, corridors, and ramps, moving always deeper into the cliff, the walls echoing with their shouts and laughter.

They came at last to the gate of the Torture Room. There had been no battles here; a dozen guards strolled around the lighted fires, and the groans and screams could still be heard.

"Unlock the gate!" shouted Zan.

The guards turned, and seeing only him and

Colin standing there, they laughed. "And who commands this?" one of them called mockingly. "Two boys?"

But as the people who followed came up behind Colin and Zan, the guards' eyes narrowed. Uneasiness and then fear crossed their faces as they saw the corridor filling with people. Among the Talmars there was no more laughter or song as they looked into the great firelit cavern. There proved no need to unlock the gates either, for as their shocked and angry cries mounted, a hundred people pressed against the gates and behind them a hundred more, until the gates burst open and the people surged in.

They cut down the men hanging over the flames and carried exhausted men from the treadmill. They broke open the doors to the cells and freed the men inside, and they stamped out the fires with their feet.

"Everyone must see this place," Colin told them. "While some of you carry the tortured men to their beds, the rest must make room for others to come in and see. When this is done let's meet in that square next to the main gates."

An hour later they gathered in the square and filled it, for the kingdom of Talmar had seven hundred citizens, and all of them had come, even the children, and all of them, having seen the Torture Room, were angry.

"Who can we name as king when all our kings turn cruel," shouted a woman, "and torture those who speak against them?"

A man leaped up and shouted, "Let's make the stranger king, the young man who came through the maze."

"Yes—the stranger," they cried, clapping.

"Well," said Zan, smiling at Colin, "you will not refuse, will you? Climb up on the platform and tell them so."

Colin walked up the steps to the platform that stood before the King's palace and listened to the cheering, enjoying it very much, because it was pleasant to be a hero. When at last it ended and there was silence in the great square, he spoke.

"My friend Zan tells me that you people of Talmar have always lived under cruel kings," he called out. "Now that you have seen what a king's power can do, isn't it time to ask yourselves why you need a king? Why don't you rule yourselves, choosing a few leaders to serve you rather than serving a king? For if your people long ago came through the maze—as I have—then once you had no king at all."

His words met with a startled silence; this was not what the people had expected to hear and they stared at him in astonishment. A low buzzing of voices began and then suddenly someone laughed. Faces turned curiously to the man who had laughed: He was an old man with one leg who leaned on a crutch.

"The boy speaks truth," he called out. "You know I came here a stranger long before my beard turned white and was sentenced to the Torture Room for six days, where I lost a leg but not my life. Now I, Kindreth, will tell you where I came from, which I have never done before. I came from the country on the other side of the maze, and there are truly no kings there, no kings at all."

There was a thoughtful silence at this until Shang, who had been captain of the guards, leaped to the platform and cried, "People of Talmar, at this moment—kingless—we are free. Do you realize this—that we are *free?* Let's have a great celebration in the square, each of us bringing what food we can, and for the first time in our lives meet together without fear."

"Without fear," echoed Zan in a voice of wonder, and Colin, looking at him, saw there were tears in his eyes.

Colin had heard Zan speak of the Talmars' cruel history, and he had seen for himself men tortured over the fires—indeed, he had come near to joining them—but it was not until he saw the tears in Zan's eyes that he really understood what it must have been like to live every moment of one's life in fear. But not only Zan was crying; all over the square tears were streaming down the faces of grown men, and women were openly sobbing.

"At sunset!" cried a girl joyously. "Celebration at sunset!"

They began to disperse to their homes in the cliff to gather up bits of rabbit meat and thin wafers of bread and herbs from the desert.

❀　❀　❀　❀

From the King's palace they carried out huge banquet tables and lanterns, which they hung all around the square, and they found and brought out food such as the people had never eaten before, so that they understood how well the King had lived at their expense. When at last they sat down to eat, there were stars in the sky, and the lanterns cast an eerie golden light over the faces at the tables. After they had eaten they talked late into the night, each citizen taking a turn.

It was a long time before Colin made them understand that he could not be their leader.

"I am truly honored," he told them, "and I confess I would love to see what happens to you all now. But I am on a long journey—the same journey, I think, that brought your Great Ones here, and I think also Kindreth as well," he said, gesturing to the old man with the crutch.

"Aye," said Kindreth, nodding, "and too old am I now to continue it, but I remember, yes."

"Perhaps, however, there are some of you who would like to come with me," added Colin, looking wistfully at Zan, who had become a rare friend now.

"But Zan is to be one of our four leaders," pointed out Shang, seeing where Colin's glance lay. "For it's agreed among us that our first leaders come from the prisoners who had the courage to want a kinder life and to suffer for it."

Zan nodded, and put out a hand to touch Colin. "I wish I might join you," he said gently. "I owe you my life, Colin, but this is my home, and never more so than now. I want to watch it change into a happier place. You understand this, surely?"

Colin nodded. "I understand."

And he did, but it went hard with him to realize that once again he must travel on alone.

6

There might be no one joining Colin on his journey the next day, but the people of Talmar rose early in the morning to collect gifts for his departure. When he woke from a long sleep, he shared food and talk with Zan. Then he walked out into the great square to find the Talmars waiting for him.

They had chosen a horse to carry him on his journey, a wild desert horse they'd tamed, with shaggy hair the color of sand dunes, and a handsome saddle of polished leather. Nor was this all. Knowing that his warm clothes had been lost in the underground rapids, they insisted that he take with him the warm fur cape that King Talmar the Eighth had worn. There was food, too—smoked rabbit meat and bread and dried herbs from the desert, and water for his leather flask, and a new woven blanket.

"You have done with kings," said Colin dryly, "but you make me feel like one."

Shang said with a grin, "But we are learning now, I think, that each one of us is a king. And because of you we burned the Rules of Xemplary last night, and today in their place we plan to write a code of honor."

"Honor?" said Colin.

"Honor," Shang said, smiling. "You have heard the word before?"

Colin grinned back at him. "It has a ring to it, yes." And he shook hands with Shang before he mounted his horse.

Zan rode with him to the gate, and there Zan gave him his own gift. "Wear this to remember me," he said, "for I will never forget you, Colin, even though we may not ever see each other again." He brought from his tunic a marvelous neckpiece from which hung chunks of rich green jade and the colored feathers—pink, orange, blue, black, white—of rare birds. "It was my father's, and his father's before him," he said. "I give it to you now, with my thanks and my blessings."

Colin was deeply touched. He buckled it around his neck and shook his head. "It's very beautiful, Zan, and I have nothing to give you in return."

Zan laughed. "Only my life, Colin. Do you count that so small a gift?" Putting out his hand he said gravely, "Good-bye, my friend." With this he tugged at his horse's reins, turned, and rode back to the square.

With a last wave Colin rode out of the gate feeling cheerful but aware, too, of an undercurrent of sadness: because he was leaving good friends behind; because across the windswept plain ahead he could still see those towering mountains, blue in the morning sunshine but very high and topped with snow; and because again he traveled by himself.

But he had a horse now for companionship, and as they rode away from the kingdom of Talmar he tried out various names on him. "Because we're going to be friends now, and you're going to need a name," he told the horse. "How do you like the name Venture?" Meeting with no response he said, "Well then, how about Talmar? Or Dune?"

The horse plodded comfortably along, paying him no attention.

"How about Hero then?"

At the sound of the word "hero," the horse pricked up his ears, lifted his head, and whinnied, causing Colin to laugh out loud. "All right—Hero it is," he said, "and now let's try you on a gallop, for we have an endless plateau to cross before we reach those mountains. But I can see a line of woods that we might reach by nightfall if we work together."

He gave Hero his head, and they galloped across the smooth turf for many a mile, with Hero showing an impressive stamina. They covered much ground, but after some miles the terrain grew stony and Colin reined in the horse, not wanting him to stumble or fall. But if the ground was stony it was also beginning to change its color, for there were patches of green here and there, and an occasional tree that the wind had twisted and combed into odd shapes.

By the time the sun had passed the top of the sky and started its journey downward, they met with a thin cluster of evergreens that encircled a spring of water.

"Here we stop and give you water and rest," Colin told Hero. "There may be some greens for you to nibble on, too. Both of us will have a picnic, Hero."

With a light heart he unpacked his food and led Hero to the spring. When the horse had drunk his fill of water, Colin tied him loosely to a tree and sat down to eat, delighted at how much easier travel was with a horse. He was seated on a rock, happily munching smoked rabbit meat, when off to the right a movement caught his eye. Startled, he put down his meat and stared. *Someone* was hiding behind a tree over there, he was certain of this, for the slender trunk of the tree did not completely conceal the man's shoulders. Colin sighed.

He was tired of fighting, he'd fought with all his might yesterday, and he was not only bone-tired of it but bored by the thought of any more. Yet there was no overlooking the fact that he was being spied upon, and he couldn't think of any happy reason for this. He shouted, "Hey over there," and reached for his slingshot and stone. "I know you're there, come out and show yourself!"

"In a minute," called a man's voice. "I'm repairing my retrovertible."

"Repairing *what?*"

A long, thin, gloomy face peered out from behind the tree, followed by a long, thin body looking like a ragbag in layer after layer of old clothes: several vests, one over the other; a sweater; a long coat; voluminous trousers; and a pair of shoes that turned up at the toes.

"My retrovertible," he said, holding up a short stick and gazing at it gloomily. "I think it's repaired now; it feels better, it looks better." He turned his glance to Colin and added, "Who might you be?"

Colin saw that his eyes were shy but friendly, and he quickly tucked his slingshot out of sight. "I'm Colin," he said, "and I don't think I know what a retrovertible is—or does," he added politely, glancing at the stick, which looked no different from any other stick cut from the branch of a tree.

"Ah," said the man, his face brightening, "a ret-rovertible does just what a retrovertible is sup-posed to do—once it's repaired, of course—and if you're Colin, then I'm certainly glad to meet you because you must be the young man who led the Talmar revolt against the King."

Surprised, Colin said, "You came by way of the Talmar kingdom? I didn't see you there—or, for that matter, see you here among the trees when Hero and I rode in, either."

The man beamed at Colin with eyes as bright as a bird's. "I? Come through the kingdom of Tal-mar? Oh dear no, I came from the other direction, through and over the mountains."

Colin said eagerly, "The mountains? You know the country I'm heading for, then? I have to confess the height of them has worried me. Can you tell me the best route to take?"

"Of course I know the country ahead," said the stranger, "and the country behind, as well as all manner of things. And I can answer any ques-tions you ask," he added with a deep bow.

"Wonderful," said Colin, "because from this distance it looks as if there's no way to get across them."

"Very tricky," the man agreed, nodding. "Steep and cold and full of storms."

"Can you draw me a map, then, of the way *you* came?" asked Colin.

"Oh, I can do more than that," the stranger said. "Is there a small hill nearby without trees?"

Colin looked at him sharply, suddenly aware of how this conversation had begun. "See here," he said suspiciously, "if you come from the opposite direction—from the mountains—how can you possibly know what happened in the Talmar kingdom only yesterday? Who are you, anyway?"

"A small hill nearby," repeated the man, looking around thoughtfully. "Ah—there we are," he said, as if Colin had never spoken, and he strode through the trees toward a rocky mound beyond them.

"I *said*—" called out Colin, and then, thoroughly exasperated, realized he was going to have to follow this peculiar man to make himself heard. "Drat the man," he muttered, and ran after him. "I asked who you are," he demanded, catching up with him, "and how you heard about—"

"Sssh," said the man, standing at the top of the mound. "Be quiet a minute and watch. I'm going to show you where the mountain pass lies that will take you through the mountains instead of over them."

"But how—"

"Sssh," he repeated.

He lifted his stick—or retrovertible, as he insisted on calling it—and flicked his wrist just as a person would snap a whip. From the stick there shot a line of the most gorgeous yellow color that Colin had ever seen; it traveled up—up—in a long curve toward the mountains, so high it seemed almost to touch the clouds in the sky before it came to rest between two jagged mountain peaks.

As Colin watched in wonder, the man flicked his wrist a second time and a stream of glorious purple followed the arc of gold, and then with another flick of the retrovertible he sent off a curve of deep rich blue and one of scarlet.

"A rainbow!" cried Colin, enchanted. "You've made a rainbow!"

The man bowed deeply, humorously. "Of course. I'm called the Conjurer," he said, "and the trail you follow lies at the end of the rainbow." With this he flicked his wrist again and the rainbow vanished.

"Oh, it's gone," cried Colin, heartbroken.

"Only so that you can try one yourself," he told him, handing Colin the retrovertible.

"I? Make a rainbow?"

"No, a rainbow has to be *built*," said the Conjurer gravely. "Go ahead, try it." He bent over Colin's wrist and showed him how to shake it. "What color would you like to begin with?"

"Green," decided Colin.

"Then think green. Think green *hard*."

Colin thought green and flicked the retrovertible; a line of pale green flowed weakly from the stick, drooped, and fell to the ground a few feet away.

"You've a very stiff wrist," said the Conjurer. "Shake 'em both and loosen 'em a bit, will you?"

Colin let his wrists dangle and shook them until they loosened. This time when he grasped the retrovertible and *thought green* a marvelous clear bright green emerged, soared to the sky, and curved into a thrilling arc. "Oh look—how beautiful!" he cried, and the Conjurer agreed that it was a handsome green.

Next Colin *thought orange;* it flew out of the retrovertible strongly enough, but instead of following the green to the east, it veered off at a right angle to the southeast, not even touching the green and messing up the rainbow. The Conjurer shook the stick and erased it. "Try again. Aim more carefully."

Colin could see that building a rainbow was not so easy as had first appeared, but his next orange followed the green, and the colors began to look like a rainbow. His red was delightful and neatly joined the others, but when he tried a purple it flew off at an angle, bumped into the other three colors, and hung there dangling, like a rope over a clothesline. It took some finagling by the Conjurer to get it down, but on the next two attempts Colin met with dazzling success: he built his rainbow, and a luxurious one it was, of yellow, orange, red, green, pink, blue, and purple.

"What wonderful fun!" cried Colin happily.

"Thought you could use some," said the Conjurer, smiling at him. "How about something to eat now?"

"Yes, of course, you must be hungry," said Colin, apologizing. "I've smoked rabbit meat we can share."

"Smoked rabbit meat sounds fine," said the Conjurer, pocketing his retrovertible, "but what would you eat if you could have anything you want?"

"Anything?" asked Colin as they strolled back toward Hero, the rainbow still hanging over them in the sky. "Oh well—roast chicken, I think, the skin all crackling brown . . . and roasted potatoes dripping with butter . . . and apple tarts, and a glass of milk, and a few cookies, and—" As they walked in among the trees he stopped in astonishment because on the spot where he'd been sitting earlier there was now a red-checkered cloth spread out on the ground. On it rested a huge roast chicken, and beside it stood silver dishes with covers and wisps of steam escaping from the corners of their lids.

He turned to the Conjurer with a gasp. "What magic!"

The Conjurer only smiled, and bringing out his retrovertible aimed it at Hero, producing a bucket of oats for him. Then he turned it on himself, and suddenly he was no longer wearing layers of ragged clothes but a very smart checked jacket and pants, a bright red plaid vest, and a pair of black-and-white shoes. "Shall we dine?" he suggested with a bow.

They sat down at once beside the picnic cloth, and Colin, feeling ravenous, ate and ate. When he'd finished, he looked at the Conjurer and sighed. "Oh, if only life could be magic like this!"

"Isn't it?" said the Conjurer, smiling. "Alive and breathing right now, aren't you?"

"Yes," said Colin doubtfully.

The Conjurer shook his head and sighed. "Folks only seem to remember the bad times, I've never understood why. *Think*," he said, and lifted his retrovertible.

At once magic moments came back to Colin, moments that he'd long since forgotten: the joy of pulling in a fish from a mountain stream as he stood in the dappled sunlight along the shore; of racing at dawn across a meadow; of learning to ride Black Prince; of skating on the ice in the winter; of schoolfriends; of the pride of making his sums come out right; and of birthdays, sixteen of them. "Yes," he said, nodding, "but like beads on a string, with long spaces in between."

"Ups and downs, ups and downs," said the Conjurer cheerfully. "Did you expect a rainbow today?"

"Of course not."

"Always unexpected," said the Conjurer, waving his fork at him to emphasize his words. "That's the way magic is."

"Is it?" asked Colin wistfully.

"Always," said the Conjurer, and then, "Always," he repeated in a fainter voice and quite suddenly he vanished. The picnic food, the oats for Hero, and the rainbow all simply disappeared, leaving Colin seated alone under a tree.

"Oh no," he cried, "it's over?" It had been so delightful that he'd completely forgotten himself. "It ended so fast," he thought, and now he was alone again, which wasn't kind at all. "How does a person hang onto such moments?" he wondered.

It occurred to him that perhaps he shouldn't have forgotten all about himself while he enjoyed the magic, that if he had remembered to hang onto himself during his enchantment he might not feel so startled and alone now. It was a strange thought, and as he untied Hero and mounted him again he turned it over and over in his mind.

"Because, Hero," he explained aloud to the horse as they rode out of the circle of trees, "I keep losing people and ending up with just myself. Perhaps I should puzzle out who this person is that I keep ending up with. What do you say to that?"

But Hero had nothing to say; he only pricked up his ears at hearing his name. Colin soon forgot what he'd said. He rode along, remembering how he'd built a rainbow and gazing at the point ahead where the rainbow had ended.

7

Hero had not taken him far beyond the circle of
trees when Colin became aware of the steady beat
of horses' hoofs pounding the earth somewhere
behind him. Startled, he reined in Hero and
turned in his saddle. It was nearing dusk and hard
to see clearly, but in the distance a figure on
horseback was galloping toward him, leaving a
cloud of dust behind. Colin watched curiously as
the figure grew more distinct and the sound became louder. Whoever it was was heading directly
toward him; as horse and rider drew nearer, the
rider waved at him, and Colin saw that he was
wearing the scarlet tunic of a Talmar.

"Who can it be?" he wondered.

And then the black horse—and it was a beautiful one—reined in beside him, and Colin found
himself face to face with a girl.

He stared at her in astonishment, seeing an
eager young face with strange, brilliant gray eyes

framed by long black hair. She said breathlessly, in a rush of words, "Last night you asked if any-one would like to travel with you—last night, back in the kingdom of Talmar. I wanted to say yes, but I didn't dare. This morning after you left I knew I had to come." She suddenly smiled at him, shyly, a little anxiously, like a child not sure of its welcome. "And here I am."

She was certainly unexpected; he wondered if she knew the dangers. She was small and surely no older than he was. He said sternly, "It's a long journey, you know, and you can't expect it to be easy because it hasn't been easy so far. Those mountains up ahead, for instance—"

She said with a little gasp, "Oh, but I'm sure that with *you* . . ."

She didn't finish, but the words gave him a very pleasant feeling. "It would be good not to travel alone all the time," he admitted. "What's your name?"

"Charmian, sister to Zan."

"Zan's sister?" he cried warmly. "But that's wonderful!" Running his eyes over the bundle tied to her saddle, he said, "Have you brought warm clothes with you?"

"Yes, and fresh meat for several days, and my stringed music maker."

That sounded sensible. "You're quite sure?" he asked. "Hero and I—that's what I've named the horse your people gave me—intend to reach that next stand of trees before darkness." He pointed ahead and then looked at her and smiled; he really had been lonely before meeting the Conjurer, and it was wonderful suddenly to have a companion.

"Then we'd better go, hadn't we?" she said.

"Good. Is your horse too tired to gallop?"

She laughed. "Just watch and see—I'll race you," she cried, and spurred her horse, setting out ahead of him and then reining in to ride beside him.

Their camp that evening was near a stream of water and proved to be a real camp, the first that Colin had experienced since he left the maze. It was Charmian who changed everything. She had brought with her a kettle, and she insisted on making numerous trips to the stream for water to heat over the fire so that they could wash themselves and their clothes. While he was cooking the fresh rabbit meat she'd brought with her, Charmian disappeared. When she emerged from the woods she carried thick branches of evergreens. These she arranged into two soft beds over which she spread their blankets. She looked fragile, but she seemed tireless as she hurried about to make him comfortable; and after they had eaten, she brought out her musical instrument to entertain him. "Have you heard any of our old Talmar ballads?" she asked.

He shook his head.

"I'll sing you a few."

How very pretty she was, he thought, watching her as she bent her head over the instrument and struck chords from its strings. She had a small heart-shaped face, and her hair shone like polished ebony in the firelight. It was certainly pleasant, he thought, to sit with her under the dark night sky with a slice of gold moon hanging above them. She sang of the desert and of the Great Ones carving out rooms in their cliff home; she sang a war song, and then a funny rhyme, and they both laughed over it.

"What did Zan say," he asked, "when you told him you were going to join me? Was he surprised? Did he send a message with you?"

"Zan?" she said with a shrug. "I left a note, that was all. He was so busy, you know."

He was disappointed, but of course Zan *would* be busy. "He'll be glad you came," he said simply. "I am."

"I am, too," she replied, smiling.

In the morning when Colin awoke he looked at his new companion across the dead ashes of the fire and saw that her eyes were open and she was looking at him.

"Hello, Colin," she said softly.

"Hello, Charmian," he said, smiling.

"I'll race you to the spring to wash," she challenged, and was out of her blanket in a second, running so fast that he couldn't catch her. They plunged into the stream together, still in their clothes, and after splashing water at each other and making a great deal of noise they sat in the sun to dry.

Sitting there they talked, and Colin told her where they were going. "I came on this journey from another country," he explained, "because I'd lost both my parents and wanted to learn the answer to such matters. This is of no importance to you, but I think you should know that I'm heading toward—looking for—a country named Galt."

"Galt," she echoed, turning the word over on her tongue.

"Yes. It could be far away. Of course, you would have other reasons for coming, but won't it go hard for you, leaving your family behind? What *did* make you decide to join me?"

She looked at him with her strange gray eyes and suddenly buried her face in her hands. "Because I think I love you, Colin."

He stared at her in amazement. "Love me?"

She nodded her head. "When I saw you—in Talmar. It's the reason I came."

She looked so small and contrite that he

smiled in spite of himself. "There's no need to hide your face," he told her gently. "I'm deeply touched, Charmian—except," he added, puzzled, "surely one can't love at only a glance, before knowing a person?"

She dropped her hands and looked at him. "But I knew you at once," she told him. "You don't believe this is possible?"

Colin thought about it. "My father courted my mother a whole year before they made their vows."

Charmian laughed. "How tedious! They were not Talmars, then, who know at once what they want!"

Looking at her lovely small face, Colin said huskily, "It would be very easy to love you, I think."

"Oh—please do!" she cried happily.

He felt his heart stir with feelings he never felt before. He had resolved to treat her as a sister —as Zan's sister as well—but here was magic after all the months of pain. He said impulsively, "You should have met the Conjurer! Did you see the rainbow as you rode toward me?"

"Rainbow?" she said, frowning. "No. Did you see one?"

Colin nodded. "And met the Conjurer as well, who told me that magic always comes unexpectedly."

"You're speaking of *me!*" she cried. "Oh, how lovely!"

"Yes," he said, and then with a start he saw that the sun was well over the horizon. "Time to break camp, Charmian," he told her. "It grows late."

"It doesn't matter so long as we are together," she said trustingly, and rose and followed him back to the camp.

They rode all day, stopping only to eat cold meat and rest their horses, but still the mountains remained at a distance. It was growing colder, however, the more miles they covered, so that by afternoon Colin was wearing the King's fur cape and Charmian a long leather coat made of stitched-together rabbit skins. "When we next camp," Colin told her, "I'll make a slingshot for you, so that we can hunt fresh meat together before ours is all gone."

"I know how to set snares," she told him. "You'll not be sorry I ride with you," she added with childlike gravity, "for I have been trained well and know many skills."

He looked at her and smiled. "I'm not sorry that you ride with me."

Their horses were near to one another; she reached out her hand and for a moment their fingers touched before the horses drew them apart. It had been a long time since Colin had felt such tenderness, and once again his heart turned over.

When they set up camp late that evening the mountains looked higher and closer at last, and Colin could begin to see the cleft between two of them that the Conjurer's rainbow had touched. The foothills were outlined more clearly, too, and were perhaps only a day's riding away. "It's going to be all right," he told Charmian.

"Of course it's going to be all right," she said, joining him and taking his hand in hers.

He found it endearing the way she liked to hold his hand or to move near him to clasp it. "But I think we should reach those foothills before we do our hunting," he told her. "There'll be more game there in the thick forests. It needs only another day's travel, I think."

That night Colin kept the fire burning continuously, getting up several times to freshen it. In the morning, opening his eyes, he found Charmian watching him. "Hello, Colin," she said, smiling at him.

"Hello, Charmian," he said, smiling back at her.

He hoped she wasn't tiring, for it was indeed hard riding, but they set out early again and stopped only for a midday meal of cold meat. But now the mountains were nearer, high and majestic —frightening, too, thought Colin, if the Conjurer had not shown him the way through. They entered the foothills, riding an ancient trail bound in moss and lined by tall trees, and that night when they camped they were protected from the wind.

But not from the cold. Charmian cooked a hot stew out of the last of their fresh rabbit meat and made hot tea from the last of the desert herbs, but nothing could keep at bay the penetrating cold that rose out of the earth—and both of them had become accustomed to desert heat. They cut an extra thickness of pine boughs on which to sleep, but there were only two blankets between them, after all. Colin shivered when he went to bed, and across the fire he could hear Charmian tossing and turning. He lay there thinking of her, of how his life had been before she joined him, and of how much he had begun to cherish her.

He saw her rise and walk over to him, carrying her blanket with her. She said softly, "I'm cold, Colin."

"Yes," he said, feeling his heart quicken, and he made room for her beside him while she spread her blanket over his.

They slept that night with their arms around each other, and in the morning when they awoke Charmian said tenderly, "Hello, Colin," and her face was next to his, her strange gray eyes luminous and shining.

And Colin, his heart captured, said softly, "I love you, Charmian." And he thought, "Nothing the Conjurer produces could be magic like this!"

"So at last you love me," she murmured in a contented voice.

He nodded. "We'll get married as soon as we reach a magistrate."

"And live happily forever after," she asked, "like in all the old stories?"

"Yes," he said, laughing, "but for now let's claim a holiday and do some hunting so we have food for the mountains ahead."

"Oh, let's stay here for days and days!" Charmian cried. "Are you happy, Colin?"

He nodded solemnly. "Happier than I've ever been in my whole life!" he said, and it was true.

After breakfast Colin carved a slingshot and collected a supply of stones for it while Charmian wove snares, and then they set out to find game. They collected roots for tea and laid the snares. Colin had killed his first rabbit when the gray sky overhead startled them both by sending down the first flakes of snow. Charmian laughed to see it. "Now we'll really *have* to stay here for days, Colin!"

He stared uneasily at the sky, the snow tickling his nose as it fell. He had not expected this, and with Charmian to take care of now he was struck by worry. "We'll need a tent," he decided.

"Oh, lovely! What shall we make it of?"

They stopped their hunting and spent the afternoon preparing a shelter. In the end it was not so much a tent as a lean-to built of tree branches woven together for their roof and then covered with sheets of moss plucked before the snow covered them. They built the hut into the side of a small hill to protect them from the north wind, and when it was finished it was delightfully cozy and warm. By then the snow was falling heavily, and Colin conceded that it truly would be wise to wait until the weather changed before tackling the mountains. They would remain here, sheltered, and hunt each day instead of riding, and lay up food for the days ahead.

And so began a time of pure happiness for Colin, who felt his love for Charmian grow warmer and deeper. Just to be with her! He told her over and over how beautiful she was, and was touched by how eagerly she listened, her gray eyes fixed unquestioningly upon him. It was a delight to walk and hunt with her, and to listen to her dreamily speculate on how it would be with them when they were married, and it was—even this—very touching to him to be taken care of, as well as to care for her. The snow stopped falling after two days, and the sun turned the ground glittering white, but neither spoke of moving on. They stretched skins on a frame and sewed them together into blankets and knapsacks in which to carry food; they dried meat and smoked it, storing it for travel. But still neither Colin nor Charmian spoke of riding on, not even when rain came and they had to rebuild their hut because it leaked.

And then one day, when the weeks had stretched out into four, Colin awoke one morning and smiled at her, and whispered happily—it had become their custom now—"Hello, Charmian."

She opened her eyes and looked at him, and her strange gray eyes were suddenly opaque, so that he could see no expression in them at all. "I'll start the fire," she said, and disentangled herself from him and the blankets to kneel over the embers and blow on them. Then she went outside, and while he dressed he waited for her to return, because it had become a pattern for her to make their first meal and for him to cook their last one.

When she did not come back Colin was surprised, but he heated up the stew and made tea before going out to call her to breakfast. He had to look a great many places for her before he found her sitting in a clearing, whittling a stick with his penknife. "So there you are," he said with relief. "The food's hot and waiting."

She held up her stick to examine it. "But it's never been my habit to eat before I work," she said. "You go ahead. I'll have something later."

"But why didn't you tell me this before?" he

asked in surprise. "We've had breakfast together all this time."

She glanced off at the horizon and shrugged. "I guess it was to please you," she said.

He stared at her in astonishment; a dozen hurt words came to his tongue, but he bit them off. He turned and went back to the hut and ate alone, and then went off to inspect the snares. When he returned later it was with five rabbits slung over his shoulder, but Charmian made no offer to help skin them.

"Are you ill?" he asked.

"Ill?" she repeated, and looked at him as if he were a stranger. "No, I'm not ill."

But that evening she did not take up her music maker to sing to him; it was Colin who plucked a few chords and then silently put it away. He thought, looking at her, "She has to be ill. I must be patient and wait, and she will be gay and happy again." But there was a deep hurt in him at the way she looked at him; it was as if she had gone far away and he was an intruder, a stranger. He felt a clutch of fear.

Charmian lay in his arms that night, but it was a different Charmian now; and when he awoke in the morning, he did not say, "Hello, Charmian," nor did she say, "Hello, Colin." Once during the day he placed his hand on her forehead to see if she had a fever, but she snapped, "I told you I'm not sick!"

"Then what is it?" he pleaded. "What's wrong, Charmian?" He looked at her, bewildered. "Suddenly you're so different, you've gone away, I can't reach you."

She gazed at him with those strange gray eyes. "I'm not any different," she said. "This is me, too."

"But—" He fumbled for words that would make her see how abruptly she had changed and why he was so bewildered. "You said you loved me," he told her quietly. "Do you still?"

"Maybe," she said with a shrug. "Sometimes . . ."

He stared at her unbelievingly. She had been so warm, so ardent, so eager, but that Charmian had totally disappeared. He swore he saw contempt now in those strange gray eyes. "What have I done?" he asked. "Charmian, what's happened to us?"

"Nothing's happened unless you let it," she said coldly. "You're being rather demanding and possessive, aren't you? I'm going for a walk."

Seeing her leave the hut he felt sick with anxiety and fear. "Cabin fever," he told himself quickly. "It has to be what they call cabin fever, from being too long in such a small hut. We'll go tomorrow," he decided, "and once we're away from this place she'll be that first Charmian again."

It was not until he lay sleepless that night that he remembered how he had said "that first Charmian"—as if, he thought, examining his bewilderment, a second Charmian lay beside him now, with no resemblance at all to the girl who had followed him out of Talmar because she loved him, the girl who had so passionately hoped he would love her in return. And now he did love her, he thought miserably, and she loved him only "maybe," only "sometimes."

8

They broke camp early the next morning. Neither of them spoke. They hung two knapsacks from each horse, and into these they packed their newly smoked meat, fresh game, roots, blankets, and clothes; it would make for slower travel with the horses so heavily loaded, but it eased Colin's worry to know they were prepared for whatever might lie ahead.

As they left the hut behind and rode off into the woods, Colin sadly turned in his saddle to look back. It seemed to him that already he was living in the past and in his memories of Charmian, when the strange part of it was that she was riding beside him. It produced a grief in him that had an especially bitter edge: He had mourned his parents not so long ago, but at least he had known they were dead; now he mourned someone who rode next to him, who was still living.

It was a bright, crisp morning when they

started out, following an old trail at first and then veering south toward the cleft in the mountains that the Conjurer had shown him with his rainbow; but at noon when they stopped to build a fire the sun had vanished, swallowed up by clouds that turned the sky leaden.

"I hope it's not going to snow," said Colin.

Charmian made no answer. Bringing fresh kindling to the fire, she very carefully walked around him, taking pains not to brush against him. Colin wondered if he would ever feel warm again; her coldness equaled the cold mountain air and chilled him as deeply as any piercing north wind.

Stamping out the fire, they climbed back on their horses. Now the trail began to slant upward at a sharper tilt, and sometimes the horses slipped and stumbled on the pebbles. It was nearing early dusk when Colin glanced up from his gloomy thoughts to see a plume of woodsmoke rising among the rocks ahead, and soon the sweet fragrance of it reached his nostrils.

Charmian lifted her head and said, "A fire?"

"Yes," he said, smiling at her; and seeing that her face was pinched from cold, he forgave her not smiling back at him.

Nearing the rocks Colin gave a shout, not wanting to startle whoever camped behind them; a man strolled out to look them over, a man in a long coat, boots, and a red beard.

"Didn't expect anybody else to be traveling," he said, his glance moving from Colin to Charmian and back to Colin. "Going to snow again, it looks like. Going far?"

"Over the mountains, at least," said Colin.

"Welcome to share my fire," the stranger told them.

"Wonderful," gasped Charmian, and jumping down from her horse she hurried in among the rocks to warm her hands.

Colin tethered both horses beyond the ring of rocks and, returning, found that the stranger had made a very snug camp inside a circle of boulders. The ground here was sandy, a smooth, silky white sand that surprised him. Over the fire the man had hung a deer steak, which sizzled as it roasted. "There are deer nearby?" asked Colin.

"Now and then," said the stranger. "Welcome to eat with me."

He was hospitable, certainly, but he talked little. From him Colin learned only that he was not a traveler such as they were: He hunted game for a village that lay on this side of the mountains, to the north, and would go back when he had meat enough.

"I," said Charmian suddenly, "am a Talmar."

"Oh?" he said, chewing thoughtfully and giving her a curious glance.

"What season of the year is it here in this country?" Colin asked.

The man swallowed his mouthful of deer meat. "Month of the Stars, first month by our count since the year began."

"Full winter then," said Colin.

The stranger nodded and jerked his head toward the pile of wood. "We'll have to keep a roaring fire going this night."

Charmian rose and without so much as a glance at Colin arranged a narrow bed close to the fire, leaving him to make his own wherever he chose. He had hoped for a serious talk with her beside the fire but that was impossible now, and he would have to wait until they were alone tomorrow. But he lay awake a long time under his blanket, puzzling over the change in her, thinking how he would reason with her and win a smile from her again. When he fell asleep he was optimistic, and he slept deeply.

He awoke shivering with cold, aware of a strange and eerie silence all around him. He saw that it was morning and that the fire was dead, and he sat up, surprised that it had not been rekindled. He glanced over to the place where the stranger had laid out his blanket and saw that he was gone. He jumped to his feet to look across the dead ashes of the fire for Charmian, and Charmian, too, was gone. There was no trace of either her or her blanket.

He whispered, "Charmian?" and then in sudden fear he shouted, "Charmian? *Charmian!*"

He ran out from the circle of rocks toward the horses, shouting over and over, "Charmian! Charmian!" and then he stopped in his tracks, his heart turning into stone.

The horses were gone—her horse, the stranger's horse, and his precious Hero as well—and with them were gone all the supplies of food and warm clothing.

He stood there in shock, letting this terrible knowledge flow through him—that she had gone without a word, simply abandoning him and taking everything with her, this girl who had stormed into his life, begging him to love her, courting him, charming him, bringing him laughter and companionship and a tenderness that he saw now —like a blow across the face—had to have been false from the beginning. The brutality of it dazed him. He wandered back to the dead fire and sat down, shivering with cold. The wind was rising, and he thought numbly, "I'd better put on the fur cape," and then he realized that this, too, was gone. She had left him only the rabbit-skin blanket under which he'd slept, and the clothes on his back. And then as he sat there, bereft and cold, he saw that she had left him something more; there were two words printed in the sand: GOOD-BYE, COLIN.

He read the two words blankly, and then he read them again. With tears in his eyes he whispered, "Hello, Colin—good-bye, Colin." At this his heart opened to his anger and to his grief and to the cruelty of her, and he lay down on the cold earth and pounded it with his fists until he was breathless and spent, and then tears came and he wept, his body shuddering under the urgency of his anger.

He did not know how long he lay there, but it was the beginning of a fresh snowfall that distracted him. He lay too tired to move, and it occurred to him that if he lay there and let the snow cover him it would not be so unkind a way to die. He had already died, he thought. He could feel the deadness in him like a spring that had broken, a deadness without feeling or hope. Charmian had taken from him much more than food and a fur cape; she had taken everything.

He thought, "I had magic, and it's gone. Is there any sense in going on when there's so little meaning to it? Dear Hoveh, I loved her—truly loved her—and she's betrayed me."

Worse, he knew that she had banished him to death without so much as a pang because she had left him with neither horse nor food, and from the sound of the wind and the intensity of the snow's falling, she had left him defenseless against a heavy storm. She had never cared at all.

He lay down again and closed his eyes, his chances of survival so small that he did not even consider them. Better to give up, he thought, give up now, once and for all, than to stumble on foot, cold and hungry, through those high mountains. He felt very calm as he made his decision and waited; the snow was falling thickly and would soon cover him, but first the bitter cold would make him sleepy and he would gently sleep his way to death. He waited, eyes closed, the snow mingling with his tears on his face.

But suddenly—and very perversely—the snow began to thin, and then it stopped falling.

He opened his eyes in anger. The wind was still howling and whistling among the rocks, but the snow had stopped falling and he couldn't understand such contrariness on the part of Nature when the storm still raged all around him.

And then he sat up in astonishment, for glancing up at the sky he saw a patch of blue directly above him, and across that patch of blue sky there leaped a line of scarlet, then bright green, followed by a deep purple and an arc of gold. *He was staring at a rainbow.*

"The Conjurer!" he whispered, and he leaped to his feet to stare in amazement at this rainbow that spoke to him in the middle of a snowstorm.

Just as suddenly as it had appeared the rainbow trembled, faded, and vanished; the sky turned leaden and the snow began falling heavily again.

"The Conjurer," whispered Colin, and felt a sense of wonder.

He was not alone, then, after all.

"A rainbow," he murmured, and shook his head in disbelief. But he had seen it, he had been given a miracle, and still under its spell he thought in a flash of astonishment, "Perhaps if one sets out on such a journey there comes a time when the gods take notice, and Hoveh stretches out a hand. Perhaps there are patterns unseen and invisible all around us . . ."

As quickly as he thought this he put it aside, for it was too strange a thought to linger long. He let it fade with the rainbow because, after all, he was still cold and alone, and without Charmian.

But he knew now that he had to go on. No one who had just seen a miracle could give up.

Carefully he took stock of what was left him; turning out his pockets, he found his penknife, a few feet of rope, and the ten gold pieces. He still had his blanket. With his knife he cut two holes in it to put his arms through, turning it into a long cape; the rope he tied around the blanket at the waist. Fortunately, he had slept in his knitted cap, and he had never removed the pendant that Zan had given him—but to remember Zan was to remember Charmian, and this he must not do. Not now, not yet.

But he had a chance, he realized. His boots were still in good repair, and his ears and his body were covered, though he had no gloves for his hands. All this was scant protection in this monstrous bitter wind, but he would go on because this place was haunted now. He refused to stay and watch the snow slowly cover those two words written in the sand: GOOD-BYE, COLIN.

As he left the shelter of the rocks he saw— near the place where the horses had been tethered —a large V shape half buried in the snow. It was his slingshot—another miracle, he thought, digging it out, for it was made of hardwood, not pine, and it would be difficult to whittle another before the storm ended; he might yet kill a rabbit to eat. Looking around he also found a scrap of fur, which must have fallen from one of the saddle packs; it made a kind of mitten for one hand when he wrapped it around his fingers.

And so Colin started out to resume the journey that seemed to have begun so very long ago. He found the woods kind to him, for the tall trees filtered out some of the snow and wind; even so the snow fell so thickly it nearly blinded him, and the wind combed it into high drifts. He walked for several hours, stopping at last because he was weak from hunger. Removing the rope from his belt, he looked for rabbit tracks in the snow and set a snare. Only then did he tear branches from the trees and pile them high enough to make a clumsy shelter into which he crawled, taking sticks and damp leaves with him to dry.

In the morning there was a rabbit in the snare, but it took him a long time to make a fire by rubbing sticks together and feeding dried leaves to the tiny flame. By noon the snow stopped falling, and a feeble sun came out. Having eaten, he forced himself to go on.

It took him three nightmare days to cover the few miles to the mountain pass. He had to wade through snowdrifts as high as his shoulder, and he was always wet and always cold. He found no fresh game, either, and soon enough ate the last of the rabbit meat, even sucking the bones for scraps and juice. Only the memory of the rainbow kept him going.

When he came at last to the mountain pass his heart plunged again. He had hoped for something easier after his journey through the snows, but now he found himself looking at a devil's caldron of stone and rock climbing at steep angles

from the point at which he met it. Huge boulders
and blocks of stone stood one above the other, like
clumsy stairs built by a giant, and he could see
dangerous holes between them through which a
person could easily fall to the floor of jagged
stones below. On either side the mountains rose
sharply; the Conjurer had described it well as a
"cleft," for it was very like a knife slash through
the mountains, caused by earthquake or ava-
lanche, which the passing of time had begun to fill
with rock.

From being wet and cold for so long he
began to be tortured by a bad cough, and he decided to stop and hunt food and rest before attempting the mountain pass. He lingered for two
days before setting out again, and then it was with
dry clothes and some fresh meat tied up in his
cloak.

But when he began to climb up this river of
stones his cough was still with him, and it tired
him very much. The sun did not reach the mountain pass, although it shone in the sky, so that he
climbed in shadow, with a cold wind at his back.
Sometimes the distances between the rocks
needed long jumps, and he would have to remove
his blanket-cape lest it trip him. It was more tiring
than walking through the snow in the woods; and
on the first night, as he slept across one of the

broad flat rocks, it began to rain, and he was drenched before he could find a rock under which to shelter.

In the morning his cough was worse and his forehead hot to the touch, but this was no place to camp and he resolutely pushed on. By now he had stopped thinking or feeling; it had become a matter of placing one foot in front of the other, stubbornly, and once in a while looking back to see how high he had climbed. The top couldn't be far, he told himself, and promised himself a fire when he reached it, and something to eat, although he had no appetite for food at all. He grew hotter and hotter until it felt as if fires raged inside him; there were moments when he couldn't remember where he was or why he was there. Once he thought he saw a figure climbing ahead—it was Charmian, he was certain—and he called out in joy, but it vanished like mist and he realized his eyes had played him false. Soon he was dizzy, talking to himself and trembling with chills. He had never felt so sick in his life. He would lie down, then force himself to get up again and jump to another rock. Again he would lie down, and again he would force himself to go on.

Very near the summit he lay down and curled up in his blanket, shivering all over and incapable of another step. He thought dimly, "There was a rainbow once, wasn't there?" and then he remembered Charmian and began to call to her, but he couldn't make her hear him. Exhausted, he closed his eyes to the delirious dreams of fever. Entering into them, he thrashed out, shouting, then fell silent with chills.

Hours passed and then, through his nightmares, he became aware of voices and of a hand touching his forehead. He knew it must be part of his dream, even to the cool cloth placed over his eyes; it did not surprise him when he felt himself being lifted and carried away by unseen hands. He only thought, "I like this dream much better. I have died, and Hoveh is carrying me off to the Sky World now."

9

When Colin opened his eyes he blinked in astonishment to find that he was lying on a slab of wood covered with furs, in a dark room lighted by a single candle. He was surprised to find his fever gone, and even more surprised to discover that he was alive, although he could not remember ever feeling so tired as he felt now. He turned his head and saw a very small woman with white hair sitting beside his bed. Seeing him awake, she gave him a bright smile and put down her knitting, went to a corner of the room, and brought back a steaming cup of soup.

"But—where am I?" stammered Colin.

"Safe," she told him in a soothing voice, and lifting him she placed pillows behind him and helped him to sit up so that she could spoon soup into his mouth.

Once the cup was empty Colin was overwhelmed by drowsiness. He closed his eyes and slept again.

After this it seemed to Colin that he slept for days, as if sleep was a food he couldn't live without, and perhaps this was so, for each time he woke up he felt bruised and exhausted, like someone who had fought too many battles and lost them all. His spirit was tired. He was content to open his eyes, smile at the little old woman, and drift off into sleep again.

But there came a day—perhaps it was weeks, perhaps a month—when he awoke feeling an interest and a sense of curiosity about where he was and who these people were who came to sit by his bed, sometimes a man, sometimes a young girl, but most often the little white-haired woman who had first given him soup and told him that he was safe.

This time when he awoke there was no one in the room with him. He sat up, and then he carefully stood, testing himself and discovering that he was only a little dizzy. Once he was upright he noticed how low the ceiling was, for he could easily reach up and touch it; he found that it was rock, which surprised him, and he sat down to think about this in a muddled way. He was sitting there when the woman hurried in, and seeing him she cried, "Oh no, no, no! You must not sit up!"

"But I'm feeling better," he told her. "Soon I'll

be well enough to leave and go on with my journey."

"Leave?" she said blankly. "Go?" She placed her hand on his forehead for a minute, as if his fever might have returned. "Such nonsense! Do lie down."

"But where am I?" he asked.

"*Safe*," she told him firmly. "Safe and warm and comfortable."

As if to prove to him how safe and comfortable he was, a real dinner was brought to him soon after this, of roasted lamb and potatoes and a vegetable he'd never seen before, with mint tea to drink. After this, and in spite of not wanting at all to sleep again, he grew drowsy and slept.

When he awoke the next time—there was no way of knowing what time of the day it was, for the candle illuminated the same darkness—he was again alone, and this time he decided to walk around and do some exploring. He left his bed, picked up the candle from the shelf on which it stood, and ducking his head under the low doorway entered a dim, candle-lit corridor.

He tiptoed, not wanting the tiny lady to hurry him back to bed. Following the hall to its end, he found that it led to a stone balcony from which other rooms and hallways opened. Directly below him lay a huge cave dimly lighted by flickering candles; he realized that he must be in some fantastic cave inside one of the mountains he'd set out to cross. He looked down into the huge room, and in the dim light he could see darker objects but the room was empty of people, and he decided that everyone must be sleeping. Noticing a ladder leading down into the cave, he descended. The dark objects turned out to be long tables, and on the opposite side of the room stood half a dozen weaving looms. They must have sheep somewhere, he thought, remembering the wool that the woman always knitted and the lamb he'd eaten for dinner. He wondered where the sheep were kept.

Now, looking around, his eyes adjusting to the dim light, he noticed all the beautiful skins and furs that hung at regular intervals around the walls. He moved toward the largest one and held up his candle to admire it.

"A bearskin," he whispered, and reached out to stroke its soft, thick warmth. Feeling a draft of air around its edges, he lifted a corner to see what lay behind it.

He recoiled in shock, nearly blinded, and dropped the bearskin at once. Picking up his candle, he raced for the ladder, fleeing what he'd seen. He found the hallway to his room, replaced the candle on its shelf, and throwing himself across his bed he lay there trembling.

What he had seen was a bright sun, and daylight, and a blue sky filled with clouds racing across a mountain peak. And with this, memory came back to him, so that he remembered desert heat, and a rainbow, and the sound of a horse galloping up behind him, and a girl named Charmian who had broken his heart—but he could not bear to remember her. He twisted restlessly as if an open wound had been touched, moving his thoughts ahead and beyond to fix them on the long ordeal up the mountain pass and the fever that had nearly taken his life. But still Charmian came back to him, and those strange gray eyes that had watched him so closely when he told her how wonderful she was. Lying there he cursed memory and cursed her, too, for her betrayal.

After a while he stopped trembling, and when the tiny woman came again to sit with him he was grateful; he asked her by what name she was known.

"Yongay," she told him in her soothing, musical voice. "We're called the Despas, and we welcome you. And your name?"

"Colin," he told her.

"Co-lin?"

He shook his head. "Col-in. How did you come to rescue me?"

"We heard your shouts and screams in the night," she told him, and shivered. "It was a miracle, for if you had gone on—" She shook her head.

"It is cold beyond imagination out there. There are winds that can tear you right off the face of the cliffs, and ice that can send you sliding to a terrible death. And always—always—a cold beyond belief."

Colin lay back on the furs and nodded. "Yes—cold," he said.

"But here," she went on, "here in the caves we are safe and we are warm."

"Yes," he said, and sank deeper against the pillows and pulled the fur blanket more securely around him. He listened to her describe all the horrors that lay outside while he sipped the herb tea she'd brought him, and presently he was lulled into sleep again.

After another week he was allowed to get up, and Yongay proudly showed him the cave where the sheep were penned; he watched the weavers spinning flax and then weaving garments on the looms in the Great Room, just as his mother had done. The next day Yongay told him he might join the wood-carvers, and he went with her to the Great Room and took his place among several men seated at a long table covered with slabs of wood. It gave him a very real joy to follow the grain of wood with the carving tool, and he quickly carved a round plate from which to eat; and then, seeing two children come to watch, he smiled at them.

"I'll carve something special for you," he told them.

Slowly, carefully, he roughed out the shape of a bird, one of the small birds—a swallow with its wings in flight—and held it out to them. "Just for you," he said. "A bird."

Two pairs of eyes turned to him questioningly. The girl said, puzzled, "Bird? What's a bird?"

There was a sudden awkward silence around the table. The man working beside Colin said, "Run along, children," and he quietly removed the carved bird from Colin's hand and said, "That was a fine plate you made. Why don't you carve us another like it?"

But Colin was stunned by the realization that the two Despa children had no knowledge of birds. He kept turning this over in his thoughts all that day and coming back to it with a strange sense of sadness.

He was not invited to carve again. Instead, he was allowed to help shear the sheep of their wool, doing this with two men named Gore and Abram. But mostly he slept a great deal.

It was a long time before he noticed that it was soon after drinking the tea that he would fall asleep. He would wake from a refreshing nap and feel ready to walk through the caves, or even do some work, and then he would drink the tea that Yongay brought him and fall asleep. At first he

thought that he must be more tired than he'd realized, but it began to seem a curious thing indeed
that it was after the tea that he grew drowsy.

He decided to experiment, and the next day he
told Yongay that he wasn't thirsty and preferred
not to drink any tea. He watched her, seeing a
flash of alarm cross her face. It was gone almost
immediately; she smiled at him as if he were a
naughty child and said warmly, "Oh, my dear, you
must drink it. It's very fine tea to keep you
healthy."

He drank it, and again fell asleep almost
immediately.

The next day he stole a small wooden bowl
from the Great Room and hid it under the fur cover
of his bed. When Yongay brought his meal—he did
not eat with the others yet—he waited until she
bent over the candle at the other end of the room,
and then he emptied his tea into the bowl.

This time he did not fall asleep.

He lay and thought about this with interest.
He guessed that if the Despas divided their day into
twenty-four hours, then he had been sleeping for
half of each day, and he wondered why they
wanted him so quiet. He liked the Despas, they
seemed a gentle and friendly people, although he
lacked interest in asking their names. He was even
growing accustomed to the darkness and could
find his way around the caves now without stum-

bling. But he was also strong and capable of doing work for them; he enjoyed carving and whittling, and he knew that he could make a great many more plates and bowls for them if he didn't sleep so much. He wondered why they didn't see this.

However, when Yongay brought him tea at the next meal he drank it because it seemed easier to sleep than to lie around and think unhappy thoughts of the past. It didn't seem worth the effort to complain. Nothing seemed worth the effort, not even getting to know the Despas better.

One day, bored and unusually restless, he strolled the halls at a different hour than usual and passed a room where children were speaking. He stopped to listen. So much seemed to be kept secret from him that it didn't occur to him to walk into the room or even pass it by; he simply stood close to the wall and eavesdropped. He soon realized it was a classroom, and the children were learning lessons.

"And who are we?" asked a sweet adult voice.

"We are the Saved Ones," recited a dozen young voices in unison. "Brought to safety when our people were desperate long ago. Our enemies are the light and the sun and the cold and the wind. Our friends are the darkness, the warm fire, and our sharing with one another."

He had counted seventeen children among

the Despas but aside from smiling at them he'd had no talks with them. Something about the words he overheard bothered him deeply, as deeply as the children who had never seen a bird fly, but he didn't try to puzzle out what it was; he only walked back to his room, where he felt safe and comfortable, and slept again.

But that evening he asked Yongay if her people had ever heard of a maze.

"A maze!" she said in surprise. "How did you know? Yes, there's a maze in our history."

So the Despas, too, had come through the maze, just as the Wos had done, and Zan and Charmian's people, the Talmars, and probably even the man with whom Charmian had gone away. All of them. This disturbed him, but he put it aside, not wanting to think about it. Except— later, waking suddenly and finding the place silent, with no sounds of voices nearby, Colin felt drawn from his bed, and for some reason unknown to him he walked down the hall, descended the ladder into the Great Room, and for the second time pulled aside the huge bearskin covering the largest hole in the cave's wall.

This time he looked out on a new moon hanging in a velvety sky full of stars. He saw the Big Dipper and Cassiopeia and the Milky Way, and he gazed at them for a long time. Then he lifted the bearskin higher and walked out to stand in the

bracing cold air. There was only a small and playful wind, and very little snow. The air felt wonderful to him after the heat and closeness of the
caves, and a faint longing rose in him for something lost to him that was not Charmian. It was a
longing for what—himself?

When he stepped back into the Great Room
he saw that someone was waiting for him and
watching him, and by the light of the candle he
recognized Yongay.

"How could you?" she asked in a reproachful
voice. "What possessed you? You have to be tired,
still, or having bad dreams. Why have you done
this?"

"I was . . . curious, I guess," he admitted,
not really understanding himself why he was here.
"I can . . . still remember things."

"Yes, but we saved your life, Colin. We've
made you warm and safe and comfortable. To
look out there is dangerous. Why?"

He said angrily, "I need more work to do. It's
very dull just sitting around."

She brightened at this. "Is that all? Well
then, tomorrow you will work with us and eat
with us. Yes—perhaps you're ready for it now. Of
course, yes, you're a young man and full of energy. We'll find things for you to do, don't worry.
In the meantime, go back to bed before anyone
else learns of this."

"Why?" he asked. "What would happen?"

She shook her head, and he thought she actually looked frightened. "Just go to bed," she told him in a low voice. She was coaxing him, and he wondered why. He felt weeks of unanswered questions rising in him, but he couldn't cope with them, his head felt too thick and his thoughts woolly. He didn't even know what had drawn him a second time to the Great Room to look out at the sky; it had been some instinct that led him, certainly not a thought or a decision.

But he also thought, jolted into awareness, "I must stop drinking their tea. Something is wrong, and I can't think what it is unless I stop the tea; and after drinking it for so long, I shall have to stop it for *days* before my mind clears."

As he lay down again on his bed he thought, "She's right, too. Everything here is done for me. Have I ever known such kindness? I must be an ungrateful monster to feel this way." But still he knew he must trust himself, and it was a strange feeling to him.

Since Colin had spent weeks among the Despas and had been given tea several times a day, many days had to pass before the drowsiness that had engulfed him was dispelled. It was also hard to find ways to get rid of the tea that he now refused to drink, and there were many times in the beginning when he thought, "What does it matter?" But something deep inside him answered, so that he found ways to spill his tea on the floor or to pour it out the moment Yongay's head was turned. He had become stubborn; he had a purpose now, and it was to become clear-headed enough to discover what felt wrong here, and why he was being drugged, and what the Despas were concealing from him.

He continued to act drowsy and to lie in bed pretending sleep, and when given work he did it cheerfully, although Yongay found little more for him to do. Slowly, very slowly, his mind began to clear. There came a morning when he awoke and opened his eyes to stare as usual through the twilight to the solitary candle burning across the room, and it was now that words he'd forgotten suddenly came back to him vividly.

"If search you must," the Grand Odlum had told him, "let me give you this advice: The important thing is to carry the sun with you, inside of you at every moment, against the darkness, for there can be—will be—a great and terrifying darkness."

The words struck and shocked Colin like a bolt of lightning. "Dear Hoveh," he gasped aloud, "what have I come to? I've let the Despas take away all my strength in the name of safety and comfort, and they've nearly murdered the sun inside me."

He was incredulous. He had allowed it to

happen because it felt so good, and because he was tired of struggle and sick at heart from Charmian's betrayal. At least he had been alive inside when Charmian had abandoned him, even though she had wounded him desperately. But here in the Despas' cave he was living in a womb; for weeks there had been no need for him to think, or to do, or to make a decision. This, then, was what had drawn him back to the Great Room, to look again beyond the bearskin in spite of his drowsiness, which had come from their herbs. It was the memory of what it had felt like to be alive.

"I must go," he thought, springing to his feet. "How could I have lingered for so long? How could I have forgotten Galt and my journey?"

Yet even now, looking around him at the room that had been his home for so many weeks, he could still feel the pull of wanting to stay and never again to risk hurt, pain, or loss. He'd been happy here—happy to be safe after nearly dying and happy to be fed after being hungry. Yes, he admitted, there was a deep longing in him to be protected.

"Protected from what?" he asked himself.

He wondered suddenly if the Despa children were also given drugs in their tea to keep them from being curious about what lay outside. Certainly they were very quiet children, never running or jumping or shouting; and now that he put his mind to remembering, he had never heard a Despa laugh. There came back to him other words that the Grand Odlum had spoken. He had said, "And those who start out, being lazy, seldom reach the end."

It was time to go.

He left the room to look for Yongay, to ask for his slingshot and his blanket-cape and to say good-bye. He found the Great Room alive with activity—it was obviously daytime again for them, and he wondered how they counted time when they never saw the sun. The women were working under a feeble torch hung from the wall, and a few men were seated at a long table sorting piles of herbs. He was surprised to see that a second group of men were pouring sacks of earth into growing jars, and he realized that some of them must leave the caves in summer to gather hay for the sheep and earth with which to grow vegetables.

He found Yongay at one of the looms, and she looked up, plainly startled to see him. She gasped, "But what are you doing awake at—" and then she covered her mouth with her hands at what she'd betrayed.

He looked at her squarely, and she looked back at him, reading in his eyes that at last he knew about the drugs. He said quietly, "I've been looking for the slingshot I had with me, Yongay, and the blanket I wore when you rescued me."

"Why?" she whispered.

"Because the time has come for me to leave."

She took a step back from him and called out in alarm, "Gore—Talen—Abram—he wants to leave, the boy plans to go."

A sudden silence fell over the Great Room and the looms stilled. No one spoke, but without a word—soundlessly—the men moved with incredible speed to surround Colin. It happened so suddenly that not until the circle closed around him did Colin feel the first stir of fear.

Straightening his shoulders he said boldly, "It's time for me to leave you now and go on my way."

Yongay said, "Tell him, Gore."

Gore nodded and said flatly, "You're not going anywhere. You belong to us now."

Colin stared at him in astonishment. "How can that be? You saved my life and for this I shall always thank you, but I'm not a Despa."

"You are now," Gore said. "Whoever comes here stays. Why do you think we fed you and nursed you back to life? You're ours now, and here you stay. Forever."

10

At the finality of Gore's words the fear that had gripped Colin deepened into terror. He saw that he had never been a guest of the Despas. Gently, without force, they had been suffocating him with comfort to kill his spirit and make him one of them. Their motive had never been kindness; they wanted to possess him and mold him into another creature of darkness. And now he was trapped.

He turned and looked at each man, one by one. In the dim light of the flickering candles their faces looked carved out of wood, and their eyes were hard and shiny like polished stones. They might be short in stature and sickly pale from no sun, but these Despa men were built strong and square, with thick shoulders and muscular arms. There were ten of them encircling him like a noose—he counted them—and he had no weapon except his fists. He might succeed in wrestling one of them to the ground, but against ten he was helpless. "Dear Hoveh," he prayed, "have I no choice but to stay? Is this how it all ends?"

And then Gore made a mistake. Seeing the change in Colin's face—seeing the boldness turn into panic and then despair—the man said in a kinder voice, "It's not so bad a life here, you know; you'll grow used to it, and outside it's much worse."

"Outside," thought Colin, and suddenly he remembered the chant of the Despa children: "Our friends are the darkness, the warm fire . . . *our enemies are the light and the sun.*"

The light.

Perhaps he had a weapon after all.

If he had stopped to think, Colin might have doubted himself, but his idea arrived so quickly, bringing with it such a surge of hope, that he gave a shout. His shout so startled the men surrounding him that he was able to slip between two of them while they were still off-balance; racing across the Great Room, he snatched at the nearest animal skin hanging on the wall and flung it to the floor. Light streamed in like a rush of fire, but Colin was already tearing down a second skin, and then another and another. As he ran among them the Despas didn't even see him; they had fallen back screaming and covering their eyes, and their shouts followed him as he ran: "Stop!" "No, no!"

And Gore's anguished voice, "Oh, the light! The light!"

Only when Colin reached the last bearskin—the huge one that covered the entrance to the caves—did he glance back into the Great Room. It was brilliant with sunshine now, and the blinded Despas were crawling on hands and knees, as helpless as he had been only a moment earlier. With a final wrench Colin pulled down the last skin and put up a hand to shield his eyes. He stepped out and then fell back as the searing light struck him; he hesitated, then in desperation snatched up the bearskin at his feet and draped it over him like a tent from which he could peer out. Trailing it behind him, he hurried up the rock-strewn slope, knowing he must get away fast—before the Despas recovered.

He fled, stumbling over the rocks and tripping over the bearskin, his eyes on the ground where only a thin cover of snow now lay in the hollows. It seemed from this, and from the warm air he breathed, that spring had begun to run tender fingers over the mountainside, thawing and melting, sending up shoots of green here and there, but Colin saw little of this because his eyes still streamed with tears from the shock of day. It was a long time before he dared to stop; reaching a knoll that was shaded by a huge tree, he pushed back the bearskin to face the light at last and look around him.

He could see again. His eyes had adjusted to the light and he could see without pain, and what he saw was beautiful: He was standing at the very top of the world and looking down on green valleys far below. The peak of the mountain lay behind him; he had finished its perilous ascent, and the only mountains he could see ahead were a line of low green hills many miles away. Fertile land, too, he thought, not the yellow sand of the desert or the brown cliffs of the Talmars or the gray rocks of the barren plateau he and Charmian had crossed, but forests and meadows and a river—friendly things that rested the eyes.

From this height he watched a low cloud drift past, and as it crossed the meadows to the east it swept them with a sudden shower of rain, then moved prettily away toward the hills, trailing silvery streamers of rain behind it. He saw an eagle soar through the sky and disappear into the trees behind him. He sniffed the fragrance of earth smells and of pine needles warmed by the sun—how long it had been!—and suddenly Colin felt a wonderful joy in being alive, and with it came a sense of wonder. He remembered the Grand Odlum saying, "Your thoughts are terrible —all dark, violent, and stormy." He remembered

Charmian, too, and how sick with grief and anger he'd been, and he said to himself, "I'm bored by ugly thoughts. I'm desperately *tired* of them."

It came to him, standing there, that he could choose for himself what thoughts he might carry down this mountain with him, for if his future lay in the valleys below, then to take his past with him was to walk backward into that future, always looking over his shoulder and stumbling. There had to be something better ahead—there already was, he realized: the first green that he'd glimpsed since he rode out of the forest to meet the Grand Odlum, and after those dark womblike days among the Despas, wasn't this enough? It was as if he'd experienced death living with them and had just been reborn.

He thought, "Perhaps there are many, *many* deaths and rebirths in life before a person moves on to the Sky World." If that were so, then it had to be wrong to hang on, fight, scream, and resist instead of just allowing everything to happen.

Rolling up the huge bearskin, Colin tucked it under his arm and set off down the trail, whistling as he went. His whistling soon stopped, however, as he discovered that walking downhill—fighting to keep from sliding and slipping as the descent grew steeper—could be as tiring as hiking uphill. But he could stop often to look down at the valley or to watch the birds soar across the sky. He had no food, but he discovered water: a swift-flowing mountain stream racing down to the valley. He took off his clothes and swam in the icy pure water; and when he resumed his hike, he was whistling again.

After several hours he came to a ledge overlooking a foothill and saw smoke rising from a point below that looked no more than an hour's distance away. If it was a campfire it could mean food; and since he'd not eaten all day, he took a mental fix on its position, lining it up with a tall ragged tree that stood out above the others, and set out to find it. He reached the site just as the sun fell behind the tops of the trees, and the smell of roasting meat caused him to nearly faint from hunger. A solitary man sat nursing the fire; Colin called out to him, and when the man glanced up and smiled Colin entered the clearing.

As he walked toward him the man looked him over with humor and stood up to hold out a welcoming hand. He was a man at whom to marvel, being not young at all but still broad-shoul-dered, strong, and tall, with a good face and eyes so kind that Colin's spirit lifted just to see them. He thought, "I'd like to look like this man some-day . . ."

"Tobias is my name," he said, shaking hands, "and I doubt I've ever seen a young man look so hungry. Am I right? I'm thinking you've come a long way from the worn look of your boots, and with only a bearskin against the cold."

"I've come a long way, yes," Colin said simply.

"Aye," the man agreed, nodding. "Sit." And he carved a slice of meat for Colin at once and handed it to him, and together they ate in silence.

"Colin's my name," Colin told him, suddenly remembering his manners when he'd eaten his fill. "And that's the first food I've had since the sun went down yesterday." Or so he could only guess, having not seen the sun either rise or set when he was among the Despas. "I thank you for it."

Tobias's glance rested thoughtfully on the necklace of jade and feathers that Colin still wore buckled around his neck. "You're welcome to my food," he said, "and welcome to the fire as well, for I've only stopped here to cook my dinner and I'll be on my way again soon." He lifted his gaze from the pendant and smiled at Colin.

"You travel in darkness?" said Colin, startled.

"There'll be a full moon, and I travel often enough to know the trails." He pointed at Colin's neckpiece. "If I were you I'd hide that," he said, "for it looks a rare piece, and the valley below can be a dangerous place."

"It certainly looks peaceful from here," said Colin, puzzled.

"It's bandit country," Tobias said with a

shake of his head. "The woods are full of them, and if they see a fine pendant like yours, who's to know if they'll bargain for it, snatch it, or kill you for it?"

Colin, considerably jolted by this news of danger ahead, lifted the neckpiece and slipped it inside his shirt.

"I particularly noticed it," Tobias went on, "because I was asked to watch out for a young man named Colin who might be wearing such a neckpiece. So if your name is Colin and you've traveled as far as I think you have, I've a message for you."

Colin stared at him in astonishment. "A message? From whom?"

"Someone named Zan."

Colin cried out in surprise, "You've passed through Talmar!"

Tobias shook his head. "No, but I've been on the other side of the mountain that stands behind us—the same that you've survived crossing—and not far from the kingdom I met five Talmars out riding. It's a strange coincidence meeting you, for this Zan said he saw you many months ago and despaired of his message finding you."

"But what did he say?" asked Colin eagerly.

The man reached into his pocket and brought out a slip of paper. "I wrote it in a language I was born to and which you'd not know, so I'll just have to say it as best I can. He asked me to tell you"—he frowned over the translating—"that he was deeply alarmed to hear that a half sister of his, child of his mother by another man, was leaving Talmar to join you. He hopes she never found you because he wishes you only good things. He said she was born and bred a true Talmar, like the King himself, and that you would understand what that means."

Colin was silent; then, feeling the man's eyes upon him, he nodded. "Cruel."

"Aye, the Talmar kings have had that reputation," said Tobias, and his gaze was kind. "And did you meet her?"

Colin nodded.

"I see." He courteously dropped his eyes from Colin's face and added a log to the fire. "Being a man who travels now and then," he said at last, "what might her name be?"

Colin felt anger at Tobias's curiosity but it quickly subsided, for the man had earned an honest answer. "Charmian," he told him.

Tobias nodded, and after a comfortable silence he said casually, "Some weeks ago—in the country back of the mountains—I met a young girl in the forest who called herself Charmian. Long black hair and strange gray eyes?"

Colin felt his heart beat faster; he said in a

tight voice, "Traveling with a man with a red beard?"

"No, quite alone," said Tobias, "although she asked if I'd seen such a man and I guessed that he'd left her."

"Then she's alone?" murmured Colin, and he thought eagerly, "It's not too late, I could go back —back across the mountain—for surely she must be lonely now, and she loved me, she said she did." Concealing his eagerness, he said politely, "When I last saw her it was bitter cold, and a storm brewing. Was she well?"

Tobias laughed. It was a curious laugh. "Oh yes, she's well. No need to worry about that girl."

"Why do you say it like that?" Colin asked suspiciously.

"Because I've met a few people with eyes such as hers before," Tobias said gently. "Strange eyes—watchful and empty, as empty as their hearts and their souls. There's no conscience in such people."

Colin bowed his head, trembling. "But she was all right—all right when you left her?"

Tobias nodded, and with no expression in his voice he said, "She had fashioned a comb out of spruce wood and had discovered a pool of water from the melting snow. When I left her she was staring at her face in the pond, admiring it and dreamily combing her hair."

"I see," said Colin, and took a deep breath and lifted his head to look at the man. "Thank you," he said steadily. "There was a moment there—"

"I saw it," the man said, nodding gravely.

"Who are you," demanded Colin, "that you travel so much and see such things in people?"

"A fair question," he acknowledged. "I'm called the Magistrate."

"Do you mean, then, that you're a sort of judge?"

Tobias smiled. "I'm many things. Judge, jury, arbiter, mentor, messenger, counselor."

"Then knowing so much," asked Colin softly, "can you tell me perhaps of a country called Galt?"

He had startled the Magistrate. "Where did you hear that name?" he demanded.

"It was told me—by a man—at the beginning of my journey."

Tobias frowned over this, and then his face softened. "Then he must have thought very highly of you," he said, "for it's not a name people speak."

"It's truly a place, then?" asked Colin, his voice eager. "Have you visited it? Have you seen it? You must have, for I saw the look on your face when I asked. You *do* know, I'm sure of it."

The Magistrate laughed and shook his head. "That's not for me to say—not to anyone—and it's time I travel on. But I'm glad we've met, Colin, and I think"—he gave Colin a glance that was almost mischievous—"I have a feeling that we may meet again."

Colin said shyly, "I wish you didn't have to leave so soon. When I saw you—when I first saw you—I hoped I might look the way you do someday . . . as if you've done much living and found answers to what I must know—*will* know—one day."

"If that's the way things are with you," said the Magistrate, standing now and tying up his knapsack, "then we *will* meet again." He added quietly, "For every answer there's first of all a question. What might yours be?"

Colin thought about it, but somehow in the presence of this man all his old questions seemed childish. "I don't know," he said with a shake of his head. "Once I did, but no more."

The Magistrate nodded. "That's very promising, then." And lifting his knapsack to his shoulder, he held out his hand to Colin.

"Promising!" cried Colin. "To know less and less? How can that be?"

"Because," said the Magistrate, smiling at him, "you have to be emptied before you can be filled." And with these words, and a cheerful wave, he walked into the woods and vanished.

11

In the morning Colin awoke refreshed from a long sleep made snug by the Despas' bearskin. An early mist had drifted in around him, but a breeze was playing with it, lifting and tossing it and gently rolling it away. As Colin bundled up the bearskin and started off down the trail again, he turned over and over in his mind the Magistrate's parting words . . . that he had to be emptied before he could be filled. Emptied of what, he wondered, to be filled with what?

It was a riddle, and a strange one.

But the Magistrate had also spoken of bandits, and that was more important at the moment. Colin wished he had a knife so that he could strip and carve a new slingshot, but having none he kept an eye out for a weapon of some kind. He picked up a stout piece of wood to use as a club until something better came along, and swung it as he walked. The sun shone through the trees, sending bright gold coins of light dancing across his path; the moss was thick as a rug underfoot, and now that he was nearing the valley he could see the gleam of white birches here and there among the pines.

And then as the trees thinned he found he could look ahead and see flat ground below him, and it was as he stood looking down at this that he heard a girl's voice shout, "Help!" and then, "Help! Help!"

Colin began running, his feet pounding fast and hard down the rough trail. The voice called again, "Help!"

Colin shouted, "I'm com—" and then he fell, rolling over and over until he came to rest against a tree, furious with himself because he knew very well that he'd not tripped over a root or a stone.

"The oldest trick in the world," he thought bitterly, a string or wire stretched across the trail and a cry for help to make him run. Scooping up the bearskin, he crawled behind the tree and waited to see what people showed themselves. Bandits, of course, he thought, and swore at himself for his carelessness.

He heard the crackling of twigs, and then footsteps; peering out from his hiding place he saw two people very near his own age come to stand a few feet away and stare down the empty trail.

"But where did he go?" asked the young man.

The girl said in a low, husky voice, "He's clever, and hiding." Quickly turning her head, she glanced at the tree where Colin hid, and he ducked too late. "Hiding *there!*" she cried, pointing. "Come out, whoever you are!"

Colin hesitated and then decided to do her bidding because there were only two of them and he had seen no weapons. Standing up he said, "That was a rotten trick—you could have killed me, you know."

Both of them stared at him in astonishment.

"But you're supposed to be a bandit," cried the girl. "You don't *look* like a bandit."

"Neither do you. Are you?" he asked.

"Of course not," she told him crossly. "I'm Serena, and this is my brother Raoul."

"I'm Colin," he said, and the three of them exchanged frank glances of appraisal.

Colin saw a slender young girl dressed in a woven blue shirt and deerskin trousers tucked into high boots. Her hair was as pale as his own, cut short, her skin tanned by the sun, and her eyes almost as intense a blue as the Grand Odlum's. Her brother Raoul was older, with the same coloring of fair hair and tanned skin except that his eyes were brown and his jaw was square where hers was round.

Colin realized that he liked them, and as they looked at him they both smiled as if they liked him, too. He said, "But if you expected to meet bandits, why have you no weapons?"

Serena laughed. "We have a few—our wits, to be exact, although sometimes this brother of mine can be stubborn about using his."

"Ha," snorted Raoul. "Remember who you're speaking to, child. But tell us—we're looking for a man called the Magistrate. Have you by any chance seen a tall, broad-shouldered—"

Colin was already nodding his head. "Yes, only last night he shared his dinner with me and then left by this same trail, saying he'd travel by moonlight."

"Blast," said Serena, "we've missed him."

"You know him well?" asked Colin curiously, and when Raoul only shrugged he said, "Do you live near here?"

Raoul shook his head. "No—over and beyond," he said, vaguely waving a hand beyond the valley. "Serena, don't you think we should ask Colin to have lunch with us—such as it is—by way of apologizing?"

Her eyes kindled. "Oh, please, let's. I know we were intended to meet. I feel it."

Colin said lightly, "Well, I feel nothing but a bleeding knee where your wire tripped me; in fact, the blood is running into my boot right now."

"Then a thousand apologies as well as lunch," Raoul said. "Serena, bandage it while I remove the wire across the trail, will you?"

"No," said his sister sweetly, "*you* bandage his knee and *I'll* remove the cord across the trail."

"Vixen," he murmured, and taking out a handkerchief tore it into strips, bidding Colin sit down and pull his trouser out of his boot. "You must certainly have been running fast—a mark of true gallantry," he commented. "The cut looks clean, though." After examining it he expertly bandaged it, saying cheerfully, "I really am sorry about this, Colin. Let me know if the bandage feels too tight."

Serena returned with a length of thin rope coiled about her wrist. She said casually, "Someone is being very clumsy back there about creeping up the hill to spy on us. I think we've been seen."

"Not seen—heard," Raoul told her, "for you do make a frightful noise when you scream, Serena."

Colin looked from one to the other in alarm. "Bandits?"

"Probably. Let's find out," Serena said, shouldering a small knapsack. "We'll leave a beautiful trail for them to follow. What fun!"

Colin didn't think it much fun, but he admired their lack of concern and picked up his bearskin and followed. They moved downhill in a different direction now, away from the trail, and soon reached the level land that Colin had seen ahead. Crossing this rough, untilled ground they entered a deeper wood to the north, and after venturing some distance Raoul fell behind to walk in the rear. Colin saw that he was erasing all traces of their passage, straightening a bent twig, smoothing away a footprint left in the soft, thick moss, briefly studying any branch they had pushed aside. After he had done this for several hundred yards he said abruptly, "Here, I think."

Colin turned and saw that Raoul had stopped beneath a huge old tree. With a quickness that startled Colin he shinnied up the trunk and vanished among its leafy branches.

"You next," said Serena, smiling at him.

Colin followed, but awkwardly, climbing until he reached a branch high above the floor of the forest and opposite Raoul, who waved at him. A moment later Serena straddled the branch just below. "Here they come," she whispered.

Colin looked down, a little dizzy from this height, and saw four rough-looking men on the trail below. They were tiptoeing and peering from side to side in a way that would have seemed comical to him if he hadn't been braced for discovery. Two of them stopped to stare into the tree, but apparently the thick foliage had swallowed up all signs of them. Colin drew a sigh of relief when the first two men hissed at their companions to hurry along. A few minutes later they vanished from sight, still tiptoeing.

"Let's follow *them* now," Raoul said mischievously, and began lowering himself branch by branch to the ground.

At hearing these words Colin suddenly felt very real misgivings about these two people he'd just met. They seemed extraordinarily reckless. Where were their fears? he wondered uneasily—first the girl announcing so casually that they were being spied upon, and then their deliberately luring the four bandits into the woods, and now—quite safe from the men—their setting out to follow them. It seemed very strange to him that they could be so playful when at the very thought of trailing four bandits he felt his own stomach muscles tense with dread. Nevertheless he followed Serena down the tree, determined not to show his fear and curious, too, as to what gave these two such confidence.

"Have you done much stalking?" Raoul asked of him when he reached the ground.

"Some."

"Then you know how to move silently—good. Let's go." He led the way, ignoring the faint path the men had followed, and moving carefully and soundlessly from tree to tree. After a mile of walking they began to hear noises ahead, and it became obvious that the four men had abandoned caution; the brush crackled and snapped under their feet, and there was loud talking among them. Raoul held up a hand and they stopped, waiting. Some moments later the smell of woodsmoke drifted toward them and Raoul nodded. "They've given us up," he whispered, and dropping to the ground he gestured them to join him. In this manner they inched forward, advancing on their stomachs.

And there were the bandits. Peering over a small rise in the ground, Colin saw them sprawled out not far away, and a scruffy-looking lot they were. The man bending over the fire had a swarthy, pockmarked face, with a patch over one eye. Another stood with his head thrown back, drinking noisily from a gourd and wiping his mouth with the back of his hand. A third sat near the fire, trimming a huge steak with a sharp knife, his face hidden under a stained felt hat. The heavily bearded fourth man sat counting a pile of silver and gold coins that he had poured from a leather sack. The size of the pile made Colin catch his breath.

Raoul turned and winked at Serena and gave Colin a reassuring smile. Throwing back his head, he closed his eyes and opened his mouth. Colin jumped in shock as the roar of a mountain lion filled the woods.

The bandits also jumped in shock, their faces slack with terror. As they stood looking around them, frozen in panic, Raoul added a very authentic snarl, followed by a menacing growl, and at this the men ran for their lives, leaving behind the coins, the meat, the knife, and all their possessions.

Colin shook his head in amazement. "You are both full of tricks, I can see that—it's no wonder you carry no weapons."

Serena said calmly, "Those bandits need a few tricks played on them now and then, for they grow frightfully greedy and conceited." She stood up, brushing twigs from her clothes, and walked into the clearing.

"But how did you ever learn to imitate a lion so well?" asked Colin, following.

"You should hear his bird calls," Serena told him. "He actually talks with them, I think." Kneeling, she began scooping up the coins and pouring them back into the leather sack. "Raoul, do you suppose these belong to the village called Nembik that was robbed yesterday? If so, they'll certainly be glad to see them again."

"You'll return them, then?" asked Colin.

Serena looked surprised. "Oh yes—as soon as possible."

"Do we take their coats, too?" Colin asked,

beginning to enjoy this. "This leather one is handsome."

"Much too handsome for a bandit," commented Serena, looking it over with a practical eye. "Stolen, of course."

"We take everything," Raoul told him, "but quickly, because their greed will soon enough see them swallow their fears and they'll be back."

Colin laughed. "To discover that a mountain lion has put out their fire and stolen their coins?"

Within minutes they had picked the clearing bare and were on their way again, Serena carrying the sack of coins, Raoul the clothes, and Colin the food the bandits had abandoned. After covering a mile of ground Raoul no longer bothered to conceal their trail and they moved faster, stopping at last when they reached a sunny glade.

"I think he's going to let us eat now," Serena told Colin humorously. "Have you eaten at all since the Magistrate shared his dinner with you?"

Colin shook his head, saying with a smile, "No, and I have been mistaken for a bandit and treated very roughly, too."

She laughed. "Then you're as hungry as I am. We mustn't build a fire because the smoke will be seen, but we've fruit and bread and cheese."

"And jokes?" suggested Raoul with a grin.

It was an affectionate smile that Raoul gave

his sister, and Colin, having been an only child, envied the warmth that flowed between them. "Jokes?" he asked.

Serena nodded eagerly. "Someone dropped an old jokebook in the woods—we found it yesterday—and in spite of being rained on and half buried in the leaves, there are still a few that can be read." She abruptly sat down and dug into the small chamois knapsack she carried. "Here's a peach for you—and an orange." She handed them out absently. "You have the cheese, Raoul?"

Raoul nodded and sat down beside Colin. "And the bread."

"And here's the book," she said, bringing from the bottom of her bag a few tattered remnants of paper. She opened these and read with obvious delight, "Why does a chicken cross the road?'"

Colin grinned. "Oh, that's an old one . . . to get to the other side."

Raoul shook his head reproachfully. "No, Colin, *no!* You're supposed to say very solemnly, 'I don't know, Serena. Why *did* the chicken cross the road?'"

"All right," said Colin. "I don't know, Serena, why *did*—"

"Oh, stop," she said, laughing. "Listen to this one instead. Are you ready?"

"Braced," said Colin.

"How do you make a slow horse fast?" She glanced up at Colin and her brother, and beamed at them. "Answer: You stop feeding him! All right —last joke: What's the best way to avoid falling hair?"

"Now that one I really don't know," Colin told her. "What *is* the best way to avoid falling hair?"

Serena chuckled. "Jump out of the way fast."

Colin couldn't help himself. He rolled over laughing, as much at Serena's delivery as at the absurdity of her jokes. It seemed like years since he'd laughed, and when he sat up he felt wonderfully lighthearted. "I don't think either of you takes anything seriously at all," he said. "Scaring away bandits with a lion's roar and collecting silly jokes."

"Silly? Now you've hurt Serena's feelings," Raoul told him gravely.

"Yes, terribly," she agreed.

Colin smiled at her, noticing again the humor in her eyes. She wasn't pretty, but she had a good face, he decided, the high cheekbones, the subtly tilted blue eyes, and the too-wide mouth all arranged to give her a distinctive quality—she looked unusual. The same features in her brother were placed differently, so that he could be described as very handsome, and yet Colin thought his face the less interesting of the two.

His gaze moved beyond them to the sun filtering down through the leaves and turning the moss a brilliant emerald green; it was very still and beautiful here. The peach in his hand was golden ripe and sweet, and the bread even better than Huldah's. He thought, "Ups and downs, ups and downs—another magic moment. But this time," he vowed, "this time I place *me* in the middle of it—all rooted and here—so there won't be emptiness when it ends; I'll be filled with it instead." And he sat quietly, savoring the presence of Serena and Raoul, and listening to forest sounds: the whisper of leaves in the breeze, the flutter of a bird as it flew from one tree to another. To these were added the smells of rich earth and decaying leaves and the pungent odor of the orange peel in his hand as he stripped the fruit of its last segment.

"It's a lovely picnic," he said as he finished, breaking the silence. "I thank you for sharing it."

"It *was* good, wasn't it," Serena said, smiling, and promptly rolled over twice in the moss and sat up.

"Serena, you'll never be a lady," her brother told her.

"Oh, I think perhaps one day I will, but it scarcely matters *now*." She cupped her chin in her hands and looked at Colin. "Something's bothering you."

It was a statement, not a question, and he nodded. "The bandits," he said. "They can't possibly have come through the maze, too?"

"But of course they did," said Raoul. "Everyone is on the same journey."

Colin felt a stir of alarm, as well as the same sense of shock that had come to him in the cave of the Despas. "But to become bandits?" he said incredulously. "To rob and steal?"

Serena's voice was matter-of-fact. "People can get . . . well . . . stuck, you know. The bandits have been here a long time, not wanting others to find what they couldn't."

"But why? What happened to them?"

Raoul shrugged. "They think they failed; it's a way they were taught to think—long ago before they came through the maze—and now they've grown attached to their misery."

"Attached to their misery," repeated Colin, and he thought about this, adding wryly, "Yes, that's certainly easy to do. But *had* they failed when they turned into bandits?"

"Is Serena a lady?" countered Raoul with a smile, and reaching over he deftly plucked the orange peels from Colin's hand and dropped them into his knapsack. "Time to go," he announced, and stood up. "We're already late."

"And so we separate now," thought Colin, and wrestled with a sense of sadness at parting.

"But first we must show Colin the road," Serena told him. "The bandits avoid the road, so it's safer for traveling."

"Of course we'll show Colin the road." Raoul said, stowing cheese away in his knapsack. "I'm thinking, too, that we could arrange to meet again somewhere along the road—tomorrow at this same time, perhaps—for we'll be traveling east by then, too."

Serena applauded. "Lovely! You do have good ideas at times, Raoul."

"He does, yes," Colin said, smiling, because he knew he wanted very much to see them again. He thought, "There is something about them—a mystery, for all their openness—that even now keeps me from asking where they're going, and why they're looking for the Magistrate, and where they come from. It lies in their fearlessness, too, and the way Raoul parried my question about the bandits." He stood up with them and tucked his bearskin under his arm. "Which way is the road?"

Raoul glanced up at the sun through the trees. "This way," he said, pointing.

"How about our meeting at the village of Terro?" suggested Serena, tossing her knapsack over her shoulder and falling in behind her brother.

Colin followed as they plunged downhill once again through the trees.

"Little Herron might be better," called Raoul

over his shoulder. "Or Huan—how about Huan? That's about the right distance."

"I think Huan's perfect," said Serena, and turned and gave Colin a smile. "We'll meet at Huan, then, although of course if we should be terribly late, you mustn't wait for us but go on."

"Huan is a village?"

"Yes, about a day's walk—one of the last that lie along this road as you cross the valley. There's a stone bridge, a stream, a small market, and perhaps a dozen houses."

The woods gave way to a thin grove of trees, and beyond it Colin saw the road they had promised him. It was the first that Colin had seen since he'd begun his journey, and leaping over the ditch that ran along beside it, he walked to its center and stood there marveling. It was a wide road, its earth worn smooth from travel. There were meadows on either side of it, too—meadows white with daisies. After being so long in the woods, it rested Colin's eyes to see so much space and light and color again.

Serena said, "They call this the High Road. Jutting off from it are many narrow roads, like spiderwebs, leading to smaller villages and hamlets in the hills, but that's where the bandits live. You must take care to stay on this road all the way to Huan."

"Yes," said Colin, "for I've certainly no interest in seeing bandits again."

They walked a few more paces with him, and then Serena put out a thin brown hand. "Good-bye for a while, then, Colin," she said, smiling. "Until tomorrow?"

"Tomorrow at Huan," he told her gravely, and turned to Raoul.

Her brother gripped both of Colin's hands with his. "We'll look for you," he said, and added with a grin, "Take care to avoid falling hair and chickens that cross the road to get to the other side."

Colin laughed, and stood watching as they cut across flat meadowland toward the woods again. When they stopped at the edge of the forest and waved to him, made small by distance, he eagerly waved back. Only then did he resume walking, but this time he felt less alone for having met them, instead of more so.

But he would see them again, he remembered, and this pleased him so deeply that he spoke the words aloud: *"Tomorrow at Huan!"*

12

As Colin walked along he thought about Serena and Raoul because, in a sense, they were still with him, the flavor of them lingering, their fearlessness amazing him. He thought, "What could make people so unafraid of bandits?"

He thought, "I would be afraid of losing my courage, but most of all of losing my life, and then also my ten gold pieces, because without them I'd be a beggar." He considered this and nodded. "A very sensible reaction, too," he decided. "Anyone would be afraid of bandits." Since he was probing something that baffled him and the valley struck him as a very pleasant place to travel, he presently dropped his speculations. He passed several horse-drawn carts on the road, and the men driving them nodded courteously; one of them greeted him with a friendly wave, asking if he'd seen any bandits.

"Not here," Colin called back, and felt warmed by this brief exchange.

He walked briskly. The sun shone and sent cloud shadows drifting now and then across the hills and meadows; among the wildflowers that grew beside the road he heard the *bzzzz* of bees gathering nectar. As the afternoon wore on, however, Colin began to realize that he was still without food and that he had brought from the Despas a bearskin that was heavy to carry and hot to sleep under in the warmer climate of the valley. Serena had mentioned a market in Huan; he began to hope the village he was approaching might have a market, too, so that he might trade the bearskin for some of the things he needed. Seeing the roofs of houses ahead, he quickened his pace.

It was a small village; he counted twenty houses along the street that was tucked behind the High Road. It looked a tidy village and a friendly one, too, as he met with smiling faces. Each house was surrounded by flowers; it had been a long time since he'd seen such colors, and the sight fed his eyes. There was a store, too, with a bright yellow sign: FOOD CLOTHS SWEETZ TOBAQ. Smiling at the clumsy spelling, he walked up a pair of wooden steps into the dim interior of the shop. "Good day," said a comfortable-looking woman sorting wool behind a counter.

"Good day," he said and stopped, glancing eagerly at the neatly displayed items.

The first thing that caught his eye, as if it waited just for him, was a woven sweater of blue-and-white design hanging directly in front of him on the far wall. He thought in amazement, "This is almost exactly like the one I began my journey with, the one my mother wove for me." He walked over and ran his fingers over its rich texture, admiring and coveting it. He said to himself, "I must have this," and he thought how fine he would look to Serena and Raoul when he met them at Huan. New boots, too, he decided, seeing a whole shelf of them, well made of gleaming leather.

The woman cleared her throat. "Can I help you?"

"Yes," he said, feeling excitement grow in him, and carried his bulky bearskin over to the counter. "I'd like to trade this for food and clothing."

She looked at the bearskin doubtfully. "I don't know what I'd do with such a thing," she told him.

"It makes a wonderfully warm blanket," he said, and began unrolling it for her. "As you can see, it's in very fine condition."

"But it's warm here in our valley," she reminded him, "and nobody needs anything so heavy."

"Then surely as a rug?" he said impatiently.

She shook her head. "You'd have to find a room in this village that's even half the size of your bearskin, for you have to admit it's huge."

He said stubbornly, "Surely people from colder places pass through who might buy it."

"Only hunters," she said with a shrug, "and hunters find their own bears." Seeing the look on his face, she added, "I can offer you *something* for it, but not much. A few *emolays,* no more—and probably never get them back, either."

"If *emolays* are money, how much?"

"I could offer twenty perhaps. Since you do not know our money I'll tell you that a long loaf of bread costs one *emolay.*"

He stared at her in consternation. "And the woven sweater over there?"

"Sixty-eight *emolays.*"

His heart sank. This was beyond bearing after seeing the sweater and wanting it; and surely, he felt, he had earned it after coming so far, and his clothes so worn and shabby now. He made his decision quickly, for want of the sweater and much more. "Have you a closet or private corner I could borrow for a moment?"

Looking mystified, she pointed to a curtain hanging from the wall. "Behind there?"

"Thank you."

He found a small alcove behind the curtain

and there he fumbled with the opening of the concealed pocket in his trousers. Bringing out his ten
gold pieces he selected the smallest, and replacing
the other nine he returned to the woman and held
out the gold coin to her.

Her eyes widened in amazement, and she
gasped, "It's a long time since I've seen one of
those." She turned and called to her husband.
"Kemor, come and look at this—a gold coin!"

Colin suddenly felt conspicuous, and flushed
with embarrassment. "Look, it's all I've got except
for the bearskin," he told her. "If you'd rather not
. . . if you don't—"

Her husband came out of a room in the back
to stand beside her, a stolid man, his face expres-
sionless.

"No, no, of course we'll take it," she said eagerly, holding it up to admire. "What a soft lovely
yellow it is!"

Her husband reached out and touched it with
the tip of a finger.

"How much would it buy in your money?"
Colin asked.

She shook her head, looking troubled. "A
great deal. I tell you this because I'm an honest
woman. It would buy too much—perhaps everything in my store—so we must strike a bargain together. You tell me all you need, and I will give
you what change I can in our money to make up

the difference. You won't need too much, will you?" she asked.

"No. The new boots, the woven sweater, a blanket, a penknife, a knapsack, and food for the journey ahead. Perhaps a spare shirt as well."

She drew a sigh of relief. "Good. And when I have added those up I will give you the change in *emolays*." Again she held up the coin to the light. "So beautiful," she sighed, her eyes wistful. "One misses such beautiful things."

"Yes," Colin said, feeling impatient now. "But you had better put it away now, hadn't you . . . hide it . . . before someone comes in?"

Her husband silently took the coin from her and went into a back room. She watched him go, and turning back to Colin said sharply, "You didn't steal it, did you?"

He was feeling uncomfortable now, wanting to finish with this and be gone. "Of course not. I brought it with me through the maze."

"Oh, the maze," she said, and appeared to lose interest.

"Did *you* come through the maze?" he asked, bringing her the woven sweater, as well as cheese and bread for his journey.

She shook her head. "My father and mother did."

Pulling on a boot and taking a few steps to

test it, Colin said, "Aren't you ever tempted to go on?"

"On?" she said, puzzled. "To where? We live here, this is home. The people who pass through here from the maze are glad enough to get here. They arrive as ragged as you, except without gold —you are the first with gold."

"How many *do* pass through your village?" he asked, adding a shirt to the growing pile.

She said with a shrug, "A dozen or so a year, perhaps. Most of them settle in the valley, glad to stop at last. You've found all you want?"

"Yes," said Colin. He watched her as she added up the prices, and when she had given him his change he thanked her and said good-bye.

He left the shop with his pockets stuffed with *emolays* and his new knapsack with supplies. He was deeply pleased about this; he felt like a squirrel with enough nuts for the coming winter, fortified for whatever lay ahead and all his losses recovered now. He thought, "One need only be without to appreciate having," and in his pleasure he found himself smiling.

Perhaps it was his smile that made people stare at him as he walked down the road that led out of the village. Certainly a surprisingly large number of people seemed to have emerged from their houses to look at him—"because I'm a stranger," he thought, and he smiled warmly at each one. But none of them smiled back, which struck him as curious. When he had entered the village the people had seemed friendly enough, but now they simply stared. He tried to puzzle out the expression in their faces but it escaped him, so that it was with a sense of relief that he left the village behind and came out on the High Road again. He thought, "There'll be a moon tonight. I'll camp somewhere beside the road, and in the morning I needn't stop again until I meet Raoul and Serena at Huan."

Toward dusk he found a pleasing spot near a brook that ran under a wooden bridge. He sat down on a grassy knoll with his back against a tree, and from his knapsack brought out cheese, a loaf of fresh bread, a slice of meat, and an apple. He began to eat with deliberate slowness, admiring the patterns the water made as it flowed and rippled around the rocks in the brook; it reminded him of the turbulent underground stream in the kingdom of Talmar, and he thought, "How long ago that feels!" He began to calculate in time how long ago it might have been. The Grand Odlum had said there was no time on this journey, but the seasons had changed; and it occurred to him, if it was spring now, that he might have passed his birthday and be a year older now.

When he had finished his meal he packed

away his food, brought out the new blanket, and rolled himself into it. He lay for a few minutes listening to the murmur of the little stream and looking up at a night sky with a full moon tangled in the branches of the tree overhead; then he closed his eyes and slept.

He slept deeply, being tired, and yet with an uneasiness that brought him strange dreams, as if something deep inside spoke to him of something wrong, something left undone, some danger overlooked. Yet try as he might he couldn't wake himself, so that in his dreams he was first struggling underwater to reach the surface and then abruptly was fighting his way up a hill that was covered with thick ice that sent him sliding back at every step. His nightmares ended when a thump on his head startled him out of sleep.

He opened his eyes to discover that he had lost the night sky and the moon; he was tightly wrapped from head to foot in his blanket and was being carried upside down over someone's shoulder.

Dazed, he thought, "My head hurts. It must have banged against a tree." Then shock followed astonishment, and he was incredulous that he had slept through this. At the same time there came to him in a merciless flash the reason for such unease in his sleep. "The gold coin," he remembered, and groaned. "Dear Hoveh, what a *fool* I was to show

it and spend it. How could I have been so stupid!"
He remembered the stares of the village people
and now—too late!—understood that the expression in their eyes had been a mixture of envy, re-
sentment, and hostility. They had known, they
must have, it was what his dreams had been trying to tell him. The man had taken the coin from
his wife, gone into the back room, and had never
returned. He must have been spreading the news
all through the village that a young man was
among them who owned a gold coin. Was he
being taken back to the village?

He began to wriggle and squirm, but his
struggle came to nothing—he was too tightly
bound—and he was soon slapped across the back
for his efforts, which left him to swear at himself
helplessly for his greed and his folly. The man carrying him suddenly stopped and spoke in a low
voice, and Colin heard two other muffled voices
reply. He was lowered none too gently to a level
surface, where he was rolled over in his blanket
and roped like a steer, the cords binding his feet
and arms to his body. The surface on which he lay
came abruptly to life. It moved, it jolted, and
Colin heard the clip-clop of a horse's hoofs; he realized he was in a farm cart, trussed and tied up
and being driven only Hoveh knew where,
bounced and bumped from side to side, and struggling for breath in his dark wool prison.

The trip seemed endless; Colin guessed they drove over rough roads for four or five miles before the cart drew to a halt. The voices grew louder now, raucous and triumphant. He was lifted out of the cart and dropped to another flat surface, rolled over until he was divested of the ropes encircling him, and then rolled over and over again until the blanket fell away. Colin found that he was lying on the earth floor of a dimly lighted hut with a man standing over him who threw a long shadow.

"Off with your boots and shirt," the man said in a harsh voice, and then to others in the room, "Find any yet?"

Colin glanced swiftly around and saw two men nearby crouched over his knapsack, tossing out food and clothes. His eyes moved to a curious hand-printed sign nailed to the wall of the hut, and he read:

GAYNO'S WILD ANIMAL SHOW
Coming Soon!
EXHIBITS!! CURIOSITIES!!
Admission, 7 emolays

For his slowness Colin was hit soundly across the ears. He sat up and hastily removed his shirt, and this exposed the pendant that Zan had given him.

"Well now," said the man standing over him, his face still in shadow. "Look here, boys—a neckpiece of real jade! We've hit a rich one, all right."

"Then there's got to be more, Gayno!"

"We'll soon find out." The man tossed Colin a pair of ragged shorts and a filthy shirt. "Strip," he said, and as the man they had called Gayno turned toward the light Colin saw his face and shuddered. He had never seen a more vicious face nor one more emptied of kindness; he knew now that he'd not been taken back to the village but was among bandits.

Silently Colin handed his clothes to the man and pulled on the rags he'd been given. He watched Gayno take a knife to his new clothes and shred them, and he winced as the remaining nine coins dropped to the floor. The three men fell on them like starving men at the sight of food.

Desperately Colin tried to think of something cheerful; he told himself they would surely let him go soon, having taken everything from him that he owned; he could see no reason for them to kill him, since to whom could he betray them? Trying to believe this, he said in a loud voice, with a bravado he did not feel, "Now that you've robbed me I'd appreciate your telling me how to get back to the High Road."

Gayno stopped and stared at him, opened his

mouth, and roared with laughter, showing broken, uneven teeth; and as the men joined with him Gayno slapped his knee. "You hear that?" he gasped between guffaws. "Hear that? 'Now that you've robbed me I'd appreciate your telling me how to get back to the High Road'?"

This set them laughing again, until Colin said angrily, "Well, what more do you want from me?"

"What more?" mimicked Gayno, chuckling. "I'll show you what more." Pulling out his knife, he held it under Colin's jaw. "Walk in front of me —outside. *I'll* show you the way to the High Road all right."

This provoked even more laughter from his men. Uneasy now, Colin stood up and walked out of the hut with Gayno behind him and the point of the knife prodding him in the spine. Outside it startled him that morning had arrived: An orange sun was rising over the jungle of trees around the hut, and the temperature was warm, even hot. Off to his right he saw a village of huts similar to Gayno's, primitive and squalid, but he was directed to the left, up a narrow red-clay road and past a thin stand of trees until he was halted beside a clearing next to the road. Three long cages stood on wheels in this clearing, and among them smaller cages sat on platforms several feet above the ground. Nailed to the fence that enclosed the compound was the same sign that he'd seen in the hut:

GAYNO'S WILD ANIMAL SHOW
Coming Soon!
EXHIBITS!! CURIOSITIES!!
Admission, 7 emolays

Gayno leaned forward and opened the gate, and they entered the compound. Colin hesitated, puzzled, still not understanding, until Gayno stuck his knife in his belt, walked over to one of the small cages, and opened its door.

"In!" he said.

"*What?*" gasped Colin.

"In," he bellowed, and seeing the look on Colin's face he laughed. "You see the sign? You're my first wild animal—and wild you'll soon be, I promise you, and earn me a fortune of *emolays* and even more gold coins!"

13

Colin stood and gaped, appalled by the smallness of the cage and in shock that he was expected to occupy it. "In!" shouted Gayno.

"No," gasped Colin, pulling away. "You can't! I won't—"

"In!" bellowed Gayno, and pushed with massive hands until Colin half-fell, half-slid inside and Gayno shoved his legs in behind him. The door snapped shut, a chain rattled, a key was turned in a padlock, and Gayno strode away, opening and closing the gate behind him.

Colin thought, "I can't believe this. It's unreal."

Stunned, he watched Gayno vanish down the road. He was alone. From the jungle of trees beyond the cage there came the keening of locusts; across the clearing a bird fluttered its wings and flew away, leaving a branch swaying and dry leaves rattling. In the silence that followed Colin put out a trembling hand to test the space around him and found little. He was crouching on a small iron floor over which a layer of sand had been tossed; above him an iron roof fitted so near to his head there was no hope of standing erect. The bars on the four sides of the cage embraced him closely but left him unprotected against sun and rain, and gave him few positions in which to find comfort.

Surely, thought Colin, the man didn't plan— the idea was inconceivable—to keep him here for long.

He spent the next moments searching for positions in which he could fit his body with the least pain. He found that he could lean his back against the bars of the cage and pull his knees to his chin, but not for long because the bars soon cut his shoulders. He could crouch, but this gave him only a small rest before the muscles in his legs screamed in protest. He discovered, however, that he could lie down by curling himself into a tight ball, and this was a relief, since it meant that he might be able to sleep; he also found that he could—with difficulty—lie flat on the floor of the cage if he ran his legs vertically up the bars.

He could also sit tailor-fashion, his legs crossed under him, and he settled on this position for now. But having explored these possibilities there was nothing left for him to do but sit and stare out at the empty compound and feel wave after wave of bitterness sweep through him.

"O Hoveh," he whispered, and then he stopped, for no gods could hear him here, of this he felt certain. Only a few hours before he had been happily restored to his journey, freed of the Despas and on his way. Now he had only a few rags on his back and nothing more, not even his freedom, and at this he buried his face in his hands, shuddering under the weight of despair and terror that rose in him.

"How can anything change so quickly?" he demanded, and as anger overwhelmed him he lifted his head and made a fist at the sky, shouting, "How can it happen? How? To have come so far and endured so much—"

And he thought of what he had endured: the silence of the maze, the heat of the desert, loneliness, fear, the battle with the Talmars, the slow recovery from the loss of Charmian, the flight from the Despas. His escapes had been many. But he could see no escape from a small locked cage. Only Gayno could free him, and Gayno was as cruel as the Talmars; Colin had been able to spend his rage against the Talmars by fighting them, but there was no way to fight Gayno. He had been rendered helpless so that his rage could only consume him. He would go mad, he thought, if he wasn't freed soon.

There was bitterness, too, in knowing that he could no longer reach Huan in time to meet Serena and Raoul; he had lost even this, and it filled him with sadness that he'd never see them again. In his mind's eye he saw their vivid faces clearly; he pictured them arriving in Huan and asking if he'd been seen; he imagined them patiently waiting until they realized at last that he wasn't coming. Serena had said, "Of course if we're terribly late you mustn't wait for us but go on." They, too, would go on; after all, they were only casual acquaintances of the road and had shared no more than a picnic. They would never know what had happened to him, for certainly when they parted there had been nothing in his shabby appearance to tempt even the most desperate of bandits. How could they have guessed that he carried ten gold pieces, one of which he would foolishly spend in bandit country?

"Fool—*fool*," he raged at himself, and then he transferred his rage to Gayno and rattled the bars of the cage as if he might tear them loose with his hands.

He thought again, "I shall go mad if they don't free me soon," and he wept and gripped the bars in despair.

The sun moved higher in the sky and beat down on the iron roof of the cage, broiling his flesh. The muscles in his legs tortured him, and he changed from sitting tailor-fashion to leaning against the bars of the cage, and then to crouching, and again to sitting, until finally he curled up into a ball on the hot floor and found a brief release in sleep.

He woke from this exhausted nap when a sharp object hit him hard on the shoulder. He opened his eyes to find the cage surrounded by at least a dozen men with savage faces. "Yah—he's awake now!" shouted one, and his companions laughed; Colin's waking up appeared to please them very much, and when he sat up as well it pleased them even more, for they were armed with rocks, which they began to hurl at him. Most of these bounced off the bars to the ground, being too large for entry, but one man threw a rotten tomato that splashed across Colin's face and ran down to his chin. After a few minutes another man went into the woods and brought back smaller stones to hand out among his friends, and following this there was nothing Colin could do but protect his eyes against the shower of stones that hit and stung his body.

A voice suddenly shouted, "Time, gentlemen!" It was Gayno standing at the gate. "Time's up—seven more *emolays* or it's over."

So Gayno charged money for the privilege of throwing stones at his prisoner; unbelievable, thought Colin as he watched the men turn away, muttering sullenly over Gayno's rules. Colin glanced down at his bare legs and arms and at the cuts and welts from the stones that had met their target. He hurt. For something to do he began picking up the stones that had been thrown at him, idly tossing them out of the cage until he discovered that several weren't stones at all but small chunks of hard, raw potato. They reminded him of how hungry he was and how long it had been since he'd eaten. He stared at the chunks of raw potato, covered with dust and grass. He reached out a hand, brushed aside their dirt with a dirty finger, and held a piece to his lips, testing it against his tongue. Yes, it was food.

He had intended to hurl out the potatoes with the stones, but he ate them instead, chewing each piece carefully to make it last and licking his fingers afterward. He felt that he must be inhabiting some terrible nightmare and that he would soon wake up beside that brook, wrapped in his new blanket, his gold pieces intact, his knapsack pillowed under his head.

It was that evening that the mountain lion arrived.

During the afternoon there had been more people who paid seven *emolays* to look at Colin and to throw stones and rotten fruit at him, enough people to cause Colin to wonder how many villagers there were in this place. But he did not wonder much: The sun and the terrible heat drove him wild, and this time when stones were thrown into the cage he picked them up and hurled them back, shouting his fury and defiance until he later wondered, in the cool of the evening, which of them had been the more afflicted by madness, he or the people who had come to torment him.

Darkness came and still Colin was brought no food or water. His stomach was growling at the unaccustomed scraps it had been given. He dreamed of cool water, of cheese and milk and rich soups; he remembered the roast chicken the Conjurer had produced, and wept over the memory. Worst of all, as the compound emptied, a sense of utter desolation swept over him that went far beyond loneliness because it brought with it the feeling that he mattered to no one, that he was losing all sense of being a person. There was no one to listen, no one to see him as a human being named Colin. To be treated as an object was to become one: He was an exhibit, a curiosity; price, seven *emolays.*

It grew cool after the sun set, and then cold. In his bare feet, ragged shorts, and filthy shirt Colin had begun to shiver uncontrollably when he heard the sound of sharp voices at a distance, of orders shouted. Then he saw a flickering light begin to illuminate the road beyond the fence.

The noises grew louder until men and torches suddenly emerged from behind the trees on the road. One man hurried up to the gate and opened it, leaving it wide, and from amid the crowd Colin heard growling sounds and strange shuffling noises.

As the procession reached the fence he saw that a group of men had wrapped chains around a large animal and were whipping it and dragging it to the gate. The beast was huge; when a torch was lifted it briefly revealed a tawny golden hide and a long sleek body, and Colin saw in astonishment that it was a mountain lion—a very tired lion, he thought, to have finished with roaring out his anger to be reduced like this to snarls and feeble lashings of his tail. The compound was suddenly filled with men and torches and a sense of urgency; the large cage standing across from Colin's cage was opened, and with sticks and whips the men inched the lion toward it.

He did not go easily. He fought, shaking his chains, balking, straining back, snarling, and something in Colin fought with him. But the lion was as doomed as he had been, and soon enough the animal was prodded up a ramp and into the cage, the chains snatched away as he entered. Trapped but freed of his terrible chains, the lion lifted his head and roared, and it was a sound to make the earth tremble.

"That will bring customers," said Gayno admiringly.

Colin cleared his throat. "Gayno," he called.

Gayno turned. "Yes?"

To ask was humiliating but his needs consumed him; he said, choking back his anger, "I've had neither water nor food since I came here."

Gayno said curtly, "Water you'll get in the morning when the lion gets his. Food you've already had—you eat what the customers throw at you. The better you perform, the more food they'll give you."

Colin said in a rush of fury, "You'll soon have a corpse on your hands, Gayno."

Gayno laughed. "You can easily be replaced," he said, and he walked to the fence and out of the compound. The torches and the men went with him, and there was darkness again, and silence, except for the sound of the lion padding back and forth in the cage across from him. The lion's anger was deep, thought Colin. He tried to resurrect his own but was too dispirited; he only leaned his head against the bars of his cage and wept. At his hunger. At his weakness. At his helplessness. At his lost journey, lost hopes, lost freedom. He had endured one day of captivity; to think of another was unendurable.

At last, to make himself warm, he curled up in the cage like a ball, and presently, lying there, the light of a waning silvery moon touched his face. He watched it for a long time, drawing nourishment from its presence and remembering kinder nights before he closed his eyes and mercifully slept.

But all through the night he remained aware of the lion—of his pacing, his growls, his occasional roar—and Colin was uneasy. His only neighbor was a wild mountain lion.

✵ ✵ ✵ ✵

The sun rose orange again, and the cool of the night dissipated under the incredible heat that poured down on Colin from the iron roof overhead. Again the people came—women and children, too, now that a wild mountain lion had been caged for them to see—and Colin moved from irritability to sullenness and then to rage. And night came, and in the morning the sun rose again, and then it was night and morning and night again. Days passed, and weeks. He watched the moon wane and then wax full and wane again. His eyes became glazed and his body grew thin, but it was as much anger as hunger that burned away his flesh, and the scars on his forehead were not from stones but from banging his head against the bars in frustration.

But he refused madness, the one escape offered him. It lived with him every minute of the day and night, like a presence, but he fought, not allowing it entry. It was close to him constantly, tempting him with its ease. It had at times a face, a body, sometimes a tender smile, sometimes a sneer; but something in him stiffened and rejected it, some old, nearly forgotten memory—of the Grand Odlum, perhaps, or the Conjurer. He survived by hate and by anger.

But he survived.

14

There came a morning when Colin opened his eyes after a fitful, uncomfortable sleep and discovered there was no longer any energy left in him to shout or rattle the bars of his cage in rage and frustration. It was a moment very like what he'd felt after fighting the Talmar guards and soldiers all day, with Zan and the Contemptibles and the citizens of the kingdom, except that now he had more deeply exhausted himself and his fury. He felt there was nothing left; he was emptied of every emotion.

He glanced across at the lion pacing in his cage—back and forth, back and forth, restlessly and angrily. As if feeling Colin's gaze on him the lion turned his head and gave him a surly, threatening look, paced to the end of the cage, turned, looked again at Colin, and stopped, standing very still, one paw suspended. Across the space that separated them they looked at each other steadily

and curiously, and then the lion gave a low growl,
tossed his head, and resumed pacing.

Colin lowered his eyes; it was too painful to
watch the animal's desperation because it was his
own as well. He preferred this strange new calm,
knowing that it couldn't last, being only a deeper
level of exhaustion, but still it was kinder to him
than the near-madness he'd gone through at being
made captive.

"And I'm still captive," he thought, his eyes
following a bird as it soared, drifted, fluttered its
wings, and flew beyond sight in the sky. "Hope-
lessly captive."

And then a strange thing happened. With his
thoughts and his anger briefly stilled there came
to him the words:

ONLY IF YOU BELIEVE YOU ARE.

These words slipping into his head startled
him. They'd not been spoken aloud, he swore it,
yet it was as if the lion had heard them, too, for
Colin saw that he'd suddenly stopped his pacing
to stare at him.

"Hello," Colin called out softly. "Hello over
there. I see you, I feel your anger. Did you hear
them, too, those words?"

The lion languidly squeezed his eyes shut
and then open again. It was not a blink but some-

thing like an acknowledgment of Colin's voice; the animal lay down and began to seriously lick his paws, but every now and then he lifted his head to observe Colin. It was as if each had been so immersed in himself that neither had noticed the other until now; certainly it was the first time since entering the cage that Colin had thought of anyone outside of himself, and it rested him to look at the lion.

But he thought, too, of the words that had so inexplicably surfaced in his mind: He was not a captive unless he believed he was. He tried out the sound of it. "I am not a captive," he said aloud. His legs hurt, his hair was filthy and matted, his eyes red-rimmed and sore, his stomach empty, he was trapped and helpless—yet he was not a captive?

By noontime the people collected again around the cages to taunt and laugh and throw things at Colin, and his fury and helplessness mounted as before until despair filled him, except now he was doubly aware of the cramped muscles in his body and the screaming tension in his legs. He shouted back at his tormentors or sank into apathy, glaring, while across from him the lion roared and snarled at the sticks prodded through the bars of his cage to tease him.

But this time when the people left and quiet came over the compound, Colin wearily lifted his head to look at the lion; he found the animal watching him.

"Another day," Colin called to him with a tired smile. "Do you think we put on a good show for them?"

The lion stretched out his long body, his tail twitching occasionally, his head up, eyes alert to the sounds of the jungle, but frequently his glance returned to Colin, and it seemed to Colin that they rested together in an oddly companionable silence.

In this silence Colin watched a bird fly out of a nest at the edge of the jungle, perch in the branch of a tree, and then fly off into the afternoon sky. He felt the stir of a faint breeze. Another bird flew out of the nest, and Colin's eyes followed it, and suddenly—watching intently the arc of its wings—he too soared free for a moment in an empty sky, with the wind at his back, and by the lifting of a wing drifted on a current of air, the earth small and green below him.

He jerked his head to clear it; what in the world was happening to him? And yet—for that moment—he had actually flown with the bird. "It's hunger," he thought. "It's making me light-headed." But a sense of discovery came to him at the same moment, and he whispered in astonishment, "Perhaps those words are true, after all. Something in me isn't captive. My thoughts can leave this cage—they just did. For a moment they carried me with them up into the sky, with the birds who are free, and for a few seconds I was free with them."

He looked over at the lion and called out to him, "Do you think we may yet go mad from all this?" The lion tossed his head and growled with such an obvious response that Colin laughed. "I like you," he called back to him. "You are the most beautiful lion I've ever seen."

* * * *

But there was nothing to assuage Colin's hunger, and his hunger gave him more pain than his cramped legs and was stronger than any experience of flying with the birds. He had become obsessed with food. In the quiet of the mornings there were usually a few birds who flew down to the ground below his cage to peck at crumbs that had fallen from people's fingers the night before. He would watch them take those precious crumbs in their beaks, and his mouth would water at the sight, for while he loved watching the birds in the sky he hated the birds on the ground for eating what could have been his, and he hated the people who carelessly dropped food that meant life to him instead of tossing it into the cage.

One day a bird startled Colin by perching on the rim of his cage and staring at him with inquisitive, beady bright eyes. Colin froze, his heart beating very fast. The bird, with foolish curiosity, hopped between the bars and came inside; and Colin, shivering from the urgency of his hunger, reached out both hands and trapped the bird, holding it captive. "Meat," he whispered. How long had it been since he'd eaten meat, he wondered, and he remembered being told that the flesh of a bird tasted like that of a chicken. He held the bird concealed against his body, grateful to whatever gods had sent him food to fill the emptiness inside him. The bird trembled in his cupped hands, he could feel its heart beating as fast as his own; his fingers curved around its neck, ready to twist and kill . . .

The bird had grown very still, waiting, and suddenly Colin was touched by its helplessness, tears coming to his eyes. He looked down at the small creature and was shaken. Lifting the trembling little bird to his cheek, he held it there for a moment and felt a wrenching, compassionate tenderness for it. Tears ran down his face as he pressed his lips against the warm feathers; he whispered, "I can't, I can't—don't ever come here again, do you hear? Don't tempt me!" Holding out his hands he opened them wide and the bird flew out of the cage and soared into the sky.

It was a different kind of helplessness that he felt now; he clung to the bars, crying weakly at his hunger and frustration until the roar of the lion distracted him. Glancing up he saw that the lion was urgently pawing at the bars of his cage and that his roar seemed to be directed at Colin.

Startled out of his misery, Colin called out, "Don't be upset. I'm sorry. It's all right now, it's all right."

The lion subsided and lay down in his cage but with his eyes fixed so intently on Colin that he smiled in spite of his tears. "Are you my nurse-maid now?" he called to him, and laughed at the absurdity of his thought.

It was the second time that he had laughed since he had been captured.

* * * *

It was the next day that Colin began to watch his thoughts with care. It came to him, sitting in his cage, that a long time ago he had stood on a mountainside looking down into this valley and he had realized that he could choose what thoughts he carried with him into the valley. He had glimpsed this in a moment of joy, but remembering how he had flown with the birds—remembering, too, that yesterday he had actually laughed aloud at the lion's imagined response—he saw that there could be truth in this.

Recalling how the Conjurer had lifted his retrovertible to bring back his happy moments,

Colin planted himself squarely in those memories, living them over again, until an hour later he found himself depressed and sad. He was astonished by this. Carefully he sorted through those memories, one by one, until he discovered that Charmian had swum in and out of his thoughts like a minnow, and following this his mind had clouded and darkened without his even noticing it.

"I must watch more closely," he vowed.

It proved the most difficult thing he had ever tried, far more difficult than making his sums balance at school. It reminded him of how he had determined not to drink the tea that Yongay had brought him when he was with the Despas, but it was much harder than that. Dark thoughts swarmed into his head like mosquitoes, too fast and clever for him to catch, and always inflicting him with pain. He was trapped . . . he would die in this cage . . . there was no hope for him at all . . . life wasn't fair, life was ugly. He began to feel like a Wo. If an angry thought drifted into his head, he soon found himself shaking the bars of the cage in fury. If a hopeless thought arrived, he would find himself staring at his emaciated arms and legs and wondering despondently how much longer he could survive. If a yearning thought intruded itself, he would think of all the people in the world enjoying themselves while he was slowly wasting away from hunger, banished and forgotten.

Yet it was a revelation to him as the days passed to discover how his thoughts controlled him, making him sad or angry or tired without his realizing how it happened.

"It's like a maze," he thought. "My thoughts start down a pleasant path that twists and turns until I come up against a wall and return to where I began—brooding in a cage, full of hate and hunger, my legs hurting."

"Maze," he repeated, startled, and then in astonishment, "Like a *maze?*"

And it came to him—nearly overwhelming him—"Can this be the *real* maze—and I myself the castle?"

* * * *

One day, waking at dawn, Colin opened his eyes and, still in that state between sleep and waking, glanced over at the lion sleeping in his cage. At that moment something inexplicable occurred: Colin found himself in a different place, no longer in his cage but roaming through tall grass with the sun warm against his body, and his body had taken on the form of the lion. He could lift his head and smell scents never known to him as a human being—fragrant grasses and a wind that blew across great spaces, bringing man scents and the smell of fruit ripening under the sun. In sudden joy he lifted his head and roared, and the call was answered from a hill to the north. Moments later he was looking into the eyes of a lioness, and there were two cubs playing at her side; he licked their fur and gave them each a gentle, playful cuff.

Colin jerked awake in surprise, and at that moment the lion awoke too, gave a mournful growl, and looked across the compound at Colin; they exchanged a long glance.

Without speaking aloud—without words—Colin said in his thoughts to the lion, "I shared your dream."

And across the space between them he felt the lion's reply, "Yes, now you know my loss, just as I feel yours."

"The sun was warm in your world, and the smells glorious."

"Yes."

"There is no difference between us now that we live in cages," Colin told him, sending the words silently by way of his thoughts. "And no separateness. Perhaps there never was." And he felt a deep sense of kinship with this huge tawny beast who kept him from being lonely, and he sent his gratitude across the clearing to him, no longer surprised that he could communicate with him. He realized that he had gone beyond thought, and was simply and purely alive. In this moment. Now. In this cage. And it was all that mattered; everything else had fallen away.

He remembered a Colin who had told the Grand Odlum that he had lost everything. "Not everything," he thought, remembering this. "Not anger or greed or jealousy. Not hatred, envy, pride, or bitterness."

Sitting in his cage, Colin felt the sun shining in himself as bright and as warm as the noonday sun outside; he smiled and moved his legs a little to ease their pain. He knew now the meaning of the Magistrate's riddle, and he was at peace.

15

The crowds of people came and went that day, but Colin did no more raging; it was beyond him even to pretend. His quietness made some of the people uneasy; others threw even more pebbles and stones to test and defeat his calm, but Colin continued to sit in his accustomed position, his legs crossed under him. Sometimes he gazed with interest into the faces of the people who taunted him; sometimes he watched the birds as they flew from their jungle nest across the clearing, and often he flew with them, a sense of great space inside of him.

The news of his quietness soon brought Gayno stomping into the compound to see the truth of it for himself. "What's wrong with you?" he demanded. "If you're sick you'll be replaced, you know. I'll feed you to the lion."

Colin said dryly, "It will be the first real food you'll have given him then, for he is starving, too."

Gayno shook his fist at him. "Stop sitting like a bloody statue, you hear? My customers don't pay to see statues, and you'll get no food from me if they stop feeding you."

As he strode away the lion lifted his head and growled; and Gayno, giving him a sharp look, hurried faster out of the compound. But Gayno was right, of course, for only a few grapes were tossed at Colin that day, and his sleep that night was even more restless than usual, bringing with it a strange dream. In this dream he saw Serena again, but not as she'd appeared in the forest. Her gold hair was no longer cropped short but reached her shoulders, and she wore a flowing blue gown and sandals. She was walking toward him with a warm smile and outstretched hands, and behind her he saw a valley with green meadows and houses climbing the sides of a mountain. The houses were small and trim, with red tile roofs; and among the lower ones stood a square white building with turrets, from which hung a flag with colorful designs of spirals, a snake, and a flower.

The dream faded and Colin awoke, the markings of that flag still vivid in his mind. He realized that he knew those designs; somewhere he'd seen them before, they were familiar to him, and he tried to remember where: a spiral, a snake, and a flower.

Dawn had come while he had dozed and

dreamed; the sun was striping the compound and sending out fingers of light, one of which reached his lap. He sat up and stretched, grateful for the sun's warmth. Then his gaze dropped to a bright round object placed neatly inside the bars of his cage, and he caught his breath in wonder and astonishment: It was an orange, a large and perfect orange.

He reached out and touched it, thinking he must be dreaming still, but it was real. He stared at it, and the sunshine seemed to illuminate and expand it until it shimmered with light. He thought he had never seen anything so beautiful in his life. Gently, tenderly, he picked it up, drew back its skin, and carefully peeled it, eating it slowly, segment by segment. It fed both his thirst and his hunger; its taste was ambrosial.

Yet its being there amazed him. Sleeping lightly he had heard no footsteps in the night, nor had the lion growled. Yet someone had placed the orange there, and the taste of it, as well as the mystery of its arrival, lingered all day. It fortified him against Gayno's second visit to harangue and threaten.

"Word's getting around," he told him in a cold rage. "You see how few people paid *emolays* this afternoon, you're losing me money."

"You've taken mine," Colin pointed out. "It wasn't enough?"

"Enough, enough," Gayno sneered. "Nothing's enough."

"You're a very cruel man," Colin told him frankly.

Gayno's eyes narrowed. "You can sit there and call me names, you—completely in my power, cramped in a cage with no food—you dare?"

Colin thought about this. "Well," he said slowly, "it seems strange, I confess, but it begins to feel possible that you can cage a man but not his spirit, and mine's returned to me, so that yes, I call you cruel. It's the truth, isn't it? And there's nothing you can do, is there?"

"I can kill you," Gayno shouted, taking a finger to his throat and running it from side to side. "Like that."

Colin nodded. "Yes, and then I'll be gone, but you will still be here, and nothing will ever be enough."

Gayno stared at him. "It doesn't frighten you?"

Colin shrugged. "Nothing's a misfortune unless I make it so."

Gayno growled in his throat, not unlike the lion.

"I don't understand you—you've gone mad. Twenty-four hours, I give you twenty-four hours," he said, shaking a fist, "and if you can't entertain them who come to see you"—again he drew the circle from ear to ear—"you go." He turned on his heel and walked away.

Colin sat and watched him leave, and after that he watched the shadows slowly lengthen across the compound. To the lion he called, "Everything comes to an end, just as Brother John said."

"Yes," came the lion's silent reply. "I myself grow thin and weak from hunger."

Colin was not disturbed by Gayno's words; what interested him far more was the moment and the fullness he found in it: the new young birds who now inhabited the jungle nest and were learning to fly; a scent in the air that reminded him of cinnamon. A full moon was rising in the west, the fifth since Colin had been captured, and he watched it among the trees until he became aware of the lion's sudden alertness. "What is it?" he called softly, and the reply came to him that someone was coming.

A thin, shadowy figure emerged from the darkness of the jungle, climbed silently over the fence, and moved toward Colin's cage without sound. A soft voice said, "Colin."

It was Serena's voice.

Colin said in astonishment, "It's *you* who brought the orange last night!"

The moon touched her face, and he saw that

she was wearing the same clothes he'd seen her in before but that her hair was long now and bound up by a leather thong. She smiled at him, nodding. "Yes, and seeing how things are with you, I made a pattern last night for the key to your cage. I've returned to free you." She held up the key triumphantly. "See?"

"I can't walk," he told her gently. "I'm too weak, Serena. I've not walked since the night after I last saw you."

She nodded. "I realized that. I've brought crutches, Colin, and there's a horse hidden in the woods." She had inserted the key in the padlock when he put his hand through the bars and stopped her.

He said, "Serena—"

"Yes?"

"Will the key also unlock the cage to the lion?"

She looked at him, puzzled. "The lion's cage? I've no idea."

"Try it."

Her shadowy figure moved across the clearing, and he heard the faint sound of metal against metal. She came back, wraithlike. "No, it doesn't fit the lion's cage. Why, Colin?"

He sighed. "Because I can't go free, Serena, and leave him here. I'm sorry, but it's impossible for me. I can't."

She stared at him in wonder. "So that's it," she said softly. "That's what brought me to you, that's what told me to come, *that's* what I felt."

"Felt?"

She nodded. "We had no idea what happened to you, Colin—Raoul and I—and no idea at all where you'd gone when you didn't meet us at Huan. And then some days ago—I can only describe it to you as tendrils of smoke rising into the sky from this place to tell us that someone—how can I explain it—as vibrations? We call them thought-forms."

"Thought-forms," he repeated. The Grand Odlum had used these words, and he looked at Serena and said, already knowing the answer, *"You come from Galt."*

She nodded. "Yes."

The memory of his dream came to him, and with it the designs of a spiral, a snake, and a flower; and he remembered now where he had seen those designs long ago: in the heart of the castle, inscribed on the four walls of the room that held the door to the maze. He said quietly, "When I began my journey I hoped to reach your country, but I can't leave with the lion still captive."

"It will take another day," she warned him. "I'll have to make a form of the lock to his cage and carve a key out of wood to fit it."

He smiled. "I realize that, but I can't leave

him." He shook his head. "It's impossible, even if it costs me my life."

She searched his face intently and nodded. "So be it. I'll try to hurry, Colin."

"Is Raoul with you?"

She shook her head. "No, he can leave our country only once a year." She turned and went back to the lion's cage; and the lion, after a low growl, lay down as she worked at the lock, taking its imprint in wax and holding up the pattern to Colin when she had finished. "I'll return," she called softly, and her slender dark form moved through a patch of moonlight and vanished among the shadows of the night.

She would return, yes, thought Colin, believing this, but he had not told her that Gayno's ultimatum would have expired before then, by midafternoon, long before darkness came to conceal her rescue.

It rained briefly in the morning, the first rain that Colin had seen here, and he understood that the seasons were changing again: He had arrived in spring, lived through a summer, and soon the season of color would be arriving. The shower of rain refreshed the air, but by noon the sun was hot again and the earth steaming, and people began arriving to pay their seven *emolays* to see him and the lion.

They came in swarms and continued coming, which amazed Colin until he realized that Gayno must have made it known there would be a killing today. They did not come and go as usual but staked out positions, which they guarded jealously. Some had brought picnic lunches with them, paying over and over for the privilege of waiting. A bizarre entertainment, thought Colin with a shake of his head.

The sun passed the top of the sky and began its slow descent toward the horizon. At midafternoon a murmur rose as Gayno opened the gate and entered the compound. He had dressed for the occasion, Colin noticed, wearing a clean shirt and a bright red sash at his waist, which almost concealed the long sharp knife tucked into it. He gravely walked to Colin's cage and brought a key from his pocket, obviously relishing the drama of the moment as the crowd waited, every eye upon him. He took his time, slowly turning the key, slowly removing the padlock and chains, slowly opening the door to the cage. "Out," he told Colin. "The time has come."

Colin said in a steady voice, "I don't believe I can walk, you know."

"Then crawl," Gayno told him curtly, and stalked to the center of the compound to wait for him.

Colin swung his legs over the side of the cage

and looked down at them, summoning whatever strength remained in those flaccid muscles and willing them to bear his weight. He placed his feet on the earth and stood upright, dizzy, knees trembling, but he stood. Slowly—step by step, head held high—he moved toward Gayno, who stood waiting with his sheathed knife and his cruel face. All of Colin's senses were heightened so that he felt the miracle of the sun on his back, and heard keenly the lion's restlessness, the anticipation behind the voices in the crowd, as well as the noise of a horse thundering down the road beyond the fence.

A woman suddenly screamed.

Turning, Colin saw a horse leap over the fence in one long, beautiful, flowing jump—a great dappled stallion—and riding it was Serena.

"*Stop!*" cried Serena in a ringing voice, and the crowd fell back afraid because she was swinging a rope with a weight attached to it that made a huge circle around her and a terrifying sound as it spun through the air. Reaching Gayno, she reined in her horse. With only the slightest faltering of that spinning metal weight, she handed down to Colin a pair of crutches and dismounted from her horse.

"I've come for your prisoner, Gayno," she told him, and as Colin tucked the crutches under his arms she handed him a small object. "The key to the lion's cage," she told him. "It is for you to do."

"Lion?" gasped Gayno. "You wouldn't dare."

"Don't move," she told him sharply.

The crowd, not hearing her, watched in puzzlement as Colin placed his weight on the crutches and headed for the lion's cage. When they saw him insert a key into its lock there came a horrified gasp, louder even than the sound of Serena's circling rope, and suddenly there came screams and a rush for the fences and the gate.

Colin opened the door to the lion's cage and said gently, "Hello, my friend. You're free now. Hurry . . . come out."

The lion stared at the open door and then at Colin; he took a step forward, growled, hesitated, and then leaped out of the cage and at Colin, sending him sprawling to the ground. The crowd hushed as they watched, waiting for the kill; but the lion, standing over Colin, bent his head over him instead and began to lick his face. From his prone position Colin reached out his arms and hugged the animal while into his ear he whispered, "Go quickly now, quickly! And don't stop until you reach your own country!"

"What an *act!*" cried Gayno behind them. "I've got to have this—what an act!" He took a step forward until Serena's circling rope stopped him.

"He's ours now, Gayno," Serena told him. "Colin, let's get out of here."

"Yes," said Colin, and to the lion he said, "Go now," and the lion, releasing him, leaped over the fence and vanished into the jungle beyond.

As Colin climbed to his feet again, Serena mounted her horse, still surrounding Gayno with her spinning rope. Reaching down to Colin, she gave him her hand and pulled him up into the saddle behind her.

"Now," she cried, digging her heels into the flanks of the horse. "Now, Jonquil!" and they galloped out of the compound, taking the fence again in one long, fluid motion and leaving an incredulous crowd behind.

But Gayno's shouts followed them. "Horses!" he cried. "Follow them! Hurry! Get the horses!"

16

Beyond the gate to the compound they swerved to the right, galloping through the squalid village that Colin had seen one dawn so many months ago. The road was red clay, narrow and rutted; Serena urged the horse onto the grass that lined one side of it, and they rode at breakneck speed through another small village and then another and another, with Colin clinging tightly to Serena, his arms around her waist. The road curved, slanting downhill; through a break in the trees Colin caught a glimpse of the High Road far below them. It vanished and reappeared; the road they were traveling grew steeper and leveled out; and a few minutes later they reached the High Road, which ran broad and smooth from left to right.

Serena reined in the horse and brought it to a halt. "Are you all right?" she asked, turning in the saddle to look at him.

"*Very* all right," he told her quietly, with a smile.

She drew half a loaf of bread from her saddlebag and gave it to him. "Being free is not enough—not yet," she said, reaching out to stroke the horse's mane. "We have a long way to go, Jonquil is tired, and I dare not push him too hard. Eat while we ride, if you can."

"I heard Gayno shout for horses to follow us," he told her.

She nodded. "Me, too. Off we go!" And grasping the reins again she turned Jonquil onto the High Road, riding at an easier pace to rest the horse.

Colin understood the need for the easier pace but also the odds against them should Gayno follow: the two of them riding a single horse and a long way to go, and Gayno with as many men, and presumably as many horses, as he cared to collect to overtake them. But for now it was enough for Colin just to be free of his cage, to feel the cool wind rushing at his face, to rest on Serena's competence as she leaned forward in the saddle, wisps of bright hair escaping from its bonds, her hands light but firm on the reins. It was enough just to see the sky.

But still it had been a long time since he'd eaten more than scraps of food. At best he was weak, and weaker now from his attempt to walk and from the tension of the last few hours. When they had covered perhaps ten or twelve miles on the High Road there began to be moments when the jolting of the horse became unbearable. Now and then he glanced back at the road, straight and level behind them, and seeing no signs of pursuit he yearned to suggest they stop. His world was slowly reduced to the steady thunder of Jonquil's hoofbeats and a blur of passing trees; he grew desperately afraid that he was going to faint.

His hopes for an early rest plummeted when Serena suddenly dug her heels into the sides of the horse and Jonquil's strides quickened into a gallop. Serena, turning her head, pointed to a hill on their right.

Colin turned then and saw them, too—eight men on horses pounding across a barren ridge and keeping pace with them on a parallel road. Not behind them but beside them, with only a few miles between.

"They *must* not capture Serena," he thought, and with this he bent every effort to forgetting his weakness and to thinking how they might escape Gayno—and he could see no way at all. He wished that he had some knowledge of the terrain ahead; he supposed that Serena knew it, and he remembered how cleverly she and Raoul had hidden from the bandits, but there was no concealing a horse.

"And what a horse," he thought as Jonquil

fairly flew along the road, yet at the same time he knew that no horse could sustain such a pace for long. At some unknown point the bandits would ride down from their hilltop trail to close in on them, and when this happened they would be trapped. A tired horse, an exhausted man, and a young girl against a party of angry bandits. It was not a pretty picture, and he cursed his weakness; they *must* not capture Serena.

Another mile and he saw that the hill on their right began to flatten out and empty into the valley to join with it. He saw that where this happened the High Road curved out of sight toward the depleted hills. That would be where the two roads converged, he thought, and where they would have to meet the bandits, and there was no escape from the trap unless they rode into the thick woods that lay directly ahead at the bend in the road. But the woods would be no refuge against Gayno, he knew, for when he and Serena did not appear beyond that curve the bandits would know precisely where to find them.

It was the forest that Serena chose. Ignoring the curving road, she sent Jonquil plunging recklessly straight ahead over a ditch and into the darkness of dense woods. Serena slowed the horse to a walk, and they moved through the silence of the deep forest toward a small bright clearing ahead, where the sun shone down on thick green moss; and when they reached this place Serena halted Jonquil. She said in a voice that trembled, "He can't go any farther," and she slid from the saddle to the ground.

Jonquil lifted his head and snorted, and this was when Colin saw that his lips were ringed with foam. "I see that," he said; he tried to lift a leg over the saddle to dismount, winced at the pain, hesitated, and ignominiously fell to the ground. Well, at least he had pried himself loose, he thought, lying there a moment before shakily attempting to stand. Serena had untied the saddle blanket and was covering Jonquil with it; as Colin limped over to help he saw tears streaming down her cheeks.

"Serena—crying?"

"I've f-f-f-failed," she blurted out, and suddenly leaned against Jonquil and wept.

Colin turned her away from the horse and held her gently in his arms. He said, "You cry when you've done so much and I'm wondering how I can ever thank you?"

"Th-th-thank me!" she sobbed. "They'll find us soon and take you back, Colin, and I set out to r-r-rescue you."

He could hear the horses out on the High Road now but he hoped that she couldn't. "You're tired and disappointed, but look at what we do have," he told her. "Trees and sun and a few more minutes—not to mention this half-loaf of bread."

He had diverted her at last. "B-b-bread!" she stammered. "But I brought more food than that, Colin, and clothes for you as well. How could I have forgotten!"

She drew away, lifted her hand to the saddle-bag, and stiffened as she heard voices shouting back and forth from the High Road; but when she turned her tear-stained face to Colin she was calm and her eyes flashed with humor. "I brought you *such* a red shirt, Colin—an old one of Raoul's, wait until you see it—as crimson as flames in the night. I also brought cheese and—"

They both looked up as a flock of birds darkened the sky overhead, circled in a great arc, and swooped down to fill a tree nearby, dozens upon dozens of them twittering and chirping, each branch of the great tree alive and swaying with their arrival.

"—and a flask of tea," continued Serena.

One of the birds left the great hemlock and flew closer, perching on a branch just over Jonquil's head. He gave a few friendly chirps and then broke into a song.

Colin laughed. "Hello there," he said, thinking the bird might almost be the same one that had flown into his cage, so exactly did it match in color and size.

"And the shirt," added Serena, bringing out a handful of scarlet.

Colin pulled off the filthy shirt he'd worn for months and fingered this new one. "Silk," he exclaimed.

"Yes," she said, and now, overpowering the birds' cheerful song, they could both hear the sound of horses entering the woods, the crackle of twigs underfoot, and men's voices.

"But I can't loosen the cork on the flask of tea," Serena told him, bending over it and deliberately ignoring the noises. "Help me, Colin?"

They both leaned over the leather flask, not even looking up when they heard Gayno's voice shout, "There they are—I see them! Hurry!"

They looked up only when there came a great rush of wings beating the air; all the birds were suddenly in motion again, taking off in formation and leaving the hemlock tree behind. It was a wondrous sight as they filled the sky. When the sound of their passing had gone, Colin's glance dropped to the woods around them and he started in amazement. "Look!" he cried, pointing.

Serena followed his gesture and gasped.

While they had been leaning over the flask a miracle had happened. All around them the trees had knit themselves together, bending, leaning, and merging until Serena and Colin now stood inside an impenetrable woven circle through which no human could possibly enter. Colin turned around incredulously, but nowhere could he see any point of entry; they were enclosed in a magic circle of green.

Serena gasped, "But what—how—?"

Colin reached for Serena's hand.

"I don't know," said Colin. "I only know—"

Serena nodded. "They can't reach us."

"No."

They stood silent and in awe until the spell was broken by a flutter of wings; the little bird who had sung to them had not flown off with his friends; now he, too, took wing and flew away into the woods. Through the tangled mesh of vines and branches and trees they could hear Gayno shouting orders in a fury; but although voices soon came to them from every side of the circle, and although they could hear sounds of the brush being attacked, neither Gayno nor his men appeared.

Colin limped to the great hemlock tree the birds had left and broke from it a strong V-shaped branch. "Have you a knife, Serena?" he asked.

"Yes," she said, startled, and handed him one from the saddlebag.

Colin dropped to the ground and crossed his legs under him, the only position in which he found comfort now. The light was fading into dusk, but he remembered the previous night's full moon. He said, "We've been given time to rest, Serena. Have we a long way to go? Is Galt still a great distance?"

"It lies beyond the horizon—not quite another day's ride," she said, watching him begin to shape the piece of wood with the knife. "Colin, what are you doing?"

"Making a slingshot so that I'll have a weapon."

"A weapon for what? Colin, the circle not only keeps Gayno out but us inside it as well. What do you think is going to happen?"

Colin thought about this and smiled. "I really don't know," he said, "but I think it's entirely out of our hands just now. Perhaps it always has been," he added with a sense of surprise. "Like meeting you, Serena. Like feeling that somehow I've known you forever."

She was still standing, half-listening to the sounds beyond the circle; perhaps she didn't hear him. He couldn't see her face but she said suddenly, "So be it," and sat down beside him and began dividing cheese and bread between them. "While you make the slingshot we'll picnic—but without jokes," she added, and gave him a sudden, radiant smile.

It had been months since Colin had known the luxury of lying down; and so it was that when he finished making the slingshot and stretched out on the soft, thick moss, he fell immediately asleep in spite of his determination to remain on guard. He fell asleep in the very middle of a sentence spoken to Serena. But if it was an exhausted sleep, it proved also an uneasy one, full of troubled dreams such as had come to him once before: a vague sense of danger, of something overlooked, of some means of entry for Gayno and his men that he'd not considered. The unease grew in him hour by hour until it felt almost as if it nibbled at him physically. He suddenly gasped in pain; opening his eyes he found the moon shining down on him and by its light he saw with astonishment that a small bird was pecking at the flesh of his arm. As he jerked himself awake the bird flew away into the darkness of the woods. Colin sat up, looking around him. "Serena?"

"Yes," she said, instantly awake.

He pointed to the forest. "It's time for us to go."

She, too, looked and saw by the moon's light that the circle had opened and the trees were separate again, as they had been earlier. "The men have gone!" she cried.

Colin said, "Yes, but I think they'll be back soon with torches to burn us out of the woods. It's what my dreams were trying to tell me."

Quietly, swiftly, they gathered up blanket, slingshot and stones, flask, and the reins of the horse; and with Colin leading Jonquil, they moved out of the moonlight into the dark of the forest to meet with the moon's radiance again on the High Road. "If I were Gayno," he said, glancing from left to right and speaking softly, "I would send six men ahead on the High Road to prevent our escape, and I would send one of them back to the village for more men, and for torches to set a fire."

Serena nodded and reached into her saddlebag. "I still have my circlet-mace," she said, bringing out the rope with which she'd kept everyone at bay in the compound; and mounting Jonquil, she laid it across her lap.

"So the rest is up to us," murmured Colin, but before he joined her he stood a moment beside Jonquil and stared intently into the forest, sending his thanks to the small bird in the same manner that he had sent his thoughts across the compound to the lion. Only then did he swing himself up into the saddle behind Serena, and they trotted off down the High Road in the moonlight.

Several hours later, with dawn beginning to brighten the sky, Serena turned the horse off the road toward a hill that rose sharply out of a field nearby; it was the first high ground they had met from which they might see what lay before them. The woods had thinned now, and the hill grew out of the earth like an absurd hat, round at the top, with a single tree stuck jauntily at its crest. They dismounted and led Jonquil up the hill with them, not wanting to leave him behind lest they be watched.

In the west the sinking moon was growing pale under the spreading light of the sun's rise, shadows were changing shape, and the ground mist was rolling away. As they shared breakfast, they watched the sun spring from behind the line of green mountains in the east, gleaming gold and feathered with pink clouds.

One of the shadows below them moved.

"You were right—someone has been waiting for us," Serena whispered.

"How far now to the mountains?" asked Colin.

"About fifteen miles to their base."

Colin looked at the road behind them and at the road ahead. "We can't stay here," he said.

"But isn't it a clever place to meet them?" Serena asked in surprise. "It's high ground, and we could fight them off so easily."

Colin shook his head. "You're forgetting there could be men coming up from behind us on the High Road."

Her eyes widened. "You really do think—?"

"I don't know, but in any case it would take only a few men to lay siege to this hill; they needn't actually fight us at all."

"And we have food but no water," she finished for him. "You're right, I hadn't thought of that. Oh, Colin, then what—?"

"How rested is Jonquil?" he asked her. "He has great stamina, but you know him better than I. Could he make a run for it with the two of us riding him?"

She looked at Jonquil measuringly. "I think he's recovered, yes, for he's certainly not been ridden hard since leaving the woods—and of course he's born and bred a Galt," she added with the flash of a smile.

He looked at her closely. "But what about you, Serena? It seems to me that you're growing tired."

She shook her head. "Not from traveling," she told him. "The atmosphere here is so much . . . stormier, denser, thicker than Galt's. That's all."

"Then let's go," Colin said, and grasping Jonquil's reins he led the way down the hill. "Lend me your jacket for its pockets, Serena, and I'll fill them with my stones. If I ride behind you I can do my best to stun a man from a distance; if they get close to us, you can swing your circlet-mace."

"Right," she said, and threw him such a spirited glance that he saw she was restored to her old self.

The High Road held many curves now, all of them perfect sites for ambush. The solitary man they had guessed to be lurking near the hill made no move to halt them; he had no need to, for as they passed they saw a steady plume of smoke rising to the sky and knew it as a signal. Where the road ahead lay straight and empty of trees Serena eased Jonquil's pace; at every copse and bend in the road he galloped.

They had covered some five or six miles when it happened: They rode at great speed around a curve to meet with four men on horseback planted in a line across the road.

"Take over, Jonquil!" cried Serena joyously, and gave him his head.

The great horse bore down on the line; the men facing them stood their ground until the last moment, when one of the horses reared in panic and sent his rider to the earth. Then they were flying past, and the three men still mounted spurred their horses to give chase. Turning in his saddle, Colin notched and shot a stone and saw one of their three pursuers slump.

But none of these men was Gayno.

Jonquil settled down now to an unswerving pace, his head high and muscles straining, but Colin knew they were not done with plots and ambushes if Gayno was still ahead. A few miles farther—halfway to the hills that loomed close now—the sun that had shone in their eyes vanished for a second behind the trees, and in this sudden withdrawal of light Colin saw the wire stretched across the High Road.

"Look out!" he shouted in Serena's ear.

With steady hands she lifted the reins and Jonquil soared over the obstruction in a flawless jump, met the ground again, and continued the pace without a break. But it had been close, thought Colin, imagining broken forelegs for Jonquil and a pair of broken heads for him and Serena. It was Gayno's work, of this he was sure, and he tried to guess what the man would plan next for them as they ran his gauntlet.

Behind them their two remaining pursuers kept up a steady pace, neither losing ground nor gaining. The sun was noon high and at their backs, the mountain ahead so close that Colin could see the line of a trail winding among its trees. As they rounded a last curve Serena reined in the horse, for here the High Road ended, and where the trail to the mountain began Gayno and a companion stood waiting, blocking their way.

Four men, thought Colin grimly, two behind and two ahead.

Serena brought Jonquil to a halt. "I still have my circlet-mace, Gayno," she called out, and she jumped from the horse to meet him face to face.

"But I have one too, now," shouted Gayno, triumphantly bringing out a rope to which he had attached an appalling disc of iron.

Colin moved to join Serena until he saw the two horsemen bearing down on them from the rear. He called out, "Steady, Jonquil! Hold fast!" and leaving Gayno to Serena for the moment he turned in the saddle and notched a stone to his slingshot. Jonquil stood motionless as Colin took aim. The first stone from his weapon missed; the second struck a horse, which turned and bolted in the direction from which it had come, its rider clinging to its mane.

They were now three against two, and Colin slipped from the horse to join Serena. He saw that Gayno's whirling circlet was steadily advancing on Serena while she fought to keep him at a distance. Colin knelt and took aim with his slingshot.

"Dear Hoveh—not to kill but to wound," he whispered, and let his stone fly. Its aim was true; it hit Gayno squarely in the jaw and with a cry he fell, his circlet-mace dropping limply beside him.

Serena's spinning circlet came to a rest. She said calmly, "And now we leave." Picking up Jonquil's reins, she led the horse around Gayno's companion and past a tree with strange markings blazed into its trunk.

The man made no move to stop them. "I don't understand. They're not going to follow?" Colin said in astonishment.

"No," she told him, "for this is where Galt begins—at this point where the trail starts over the mountain." Seeing his look of doubt, she added, "I don't know why it is so, but no one ever trespasses beyond its boundary. The Magistrate says it's because deep in every man there's a hope he may still find his way here."

"Even Gayno?" asked Colin, but he already knew the answer.

"Even Gayno." She reached out a hand to him, smiling. "Welcome to Galt, Colin."

"And the name of my country is Galt," the Grand Odlum had told him.

Colin stood very still, transfixed by the memory of how long ago those words had been spoken and how far he had come. He turned and looked back at the road; he saw two bandits riding across it, with Gayno tied to a horse between them, but in his mind's eye he saw far more: He saw deserts, caves, forests, cliffs, high mountains, a maze, and a cage. He saw, too, with absolute clarity, that when he reached the top of this mountain behind him he would look down on a valley that held clusters of red-roofed houses, as well as a square white building with a flag bearing a spiral, a snake, and a flower. He knew because he had seen it in his dream.

He turned back to the trail and stopped, puzzled by a change in atmosphere. "But something's different, Serena. What is it I feel?" he asked, struck by a sense of buoyancy, of calm, and of warmth.

"It's what becomes possible to anyone who breaks out of the maze," she told him, smiling. "Are you ready to go now?"

"Yes," he said gladly, and with Jonquil following and Serena beside him, he walked toward the horizon into the country of the dawn.

J
GIL

Gilman, Dorothy

The maze in the
heart of the castle

DATE			
~~JUL 16 1993~~			
~~JUL 1 9 1994~~			
AUG 20 1997			